KING

OF

I0629482

Morgan Park

Book 5 of the Kings of the Castle Series

Book 1 is the Introduction

Books 2-9 are standalones

Karen D. Bradley

Ambrosia Sands Books
Dolton, Illinois

King of Morgan Park by Karen D. Bradley Copyright ©2019

Trade Paperback ISBN: 978-1-7336089-3-0
Digital ISBN: 978-1-7336089-2-3
LCCN: 2019912508

Ambrosia Sands Books
P.O. Box 827
Dolton, IL 60419
www.ambrosiasands.com

Cover Designed by: J.L Woodson: www.woodsoncreativestudio.com
Interior Designed by: Lissa Woodson: www.naleighnakai.com
Editor: Lissa Woodson: www.naleighnakai.com

Manufactured and Printed in the United States of America

KING

OF

Morgan Park

Book 5 of the Kings of the Castle Series

Book 1 is the Introduction

Books 2-9 are standalones

Karen D. Bradley

♦ DEDICATION ♦

To all the Kings and Queens who purpose require above average sacrifice, keep doing what you're doing. People may be silent now but they are watching you as you create a legacy and leaving a mark on the world.

♦ ACKNOWLEDGEMENTS ♦

To my family and friends and core group of readers, thanks for supporting me through the ups and downs of this unexpected writing expedition. Most of what I have accomplished has been due to your excitement and encouragement that has provided fuel for a journey I wasn't sure was mine to take.

A special shout out to my sister, Jenetta M. Bradley, for her part in getting my books off the shelf where they were collecting dust. I appreciate you reading my stories over and over again without complaint.

English and Grammar were never my strongest subjects but the stories in my head didn't seem to care about that fact. Thanks to my editors Lissa Woodson (Naleighna Kai) and J.L. Campbell for your energy and efforts in strengthening the weakness in my writing, challenging me to be better and improving the novel.

To Christine Pauls, Ellen Kiley Goeckler, and Debra Mitchell, I appreciate your time and assistance. Your comments, corrections and questions were essential to putting the final touches to the story. Thank you to my Tribe.

A special thanks to J. L. Woodson for doing what you do best—creating awesome covers.

Finally, thank you to everyone who purchases a book, know your support is appreciated.

CHAPTER 1

The words *I saw Levi Diesel kill a man* broke through Daron Kincaid's sleep haze.

A wave of familiarity hit Daron as he bolted from the bed and glanced at the clock, his heart racing. Weeks ago, Katara Johnson—one of his few clients—made an early-morning call about her daughter Tracy being missing. This time, the call came from one of three young men participating in his enrichment program.

"Mr. Dee, we're in trouble," Amarion, a small-time thief replied, his voice heavy with fear. His specialty was stealing jewelry but his life's goal was to be a sculptor. Daron wanted to make sure he lived long enough for that to happen.

"Did he see you?" Daron whispered, flipping back the Egyptian cotton sheet, noting the rise and fall of Cameron's chest as he slid out of the bed.

The last time he received an early-morning call, he also got a text informing him that Khalil, the man who hired Daron's company, Crossroads Security, had been shot. Those two events were subtly interrelated. Daron pulled the cell from his ear to check for notifications. Thankfully, there wasn't another incident at The Castle.

"No, but this slim dude they call Midas, may have." The young man's shaky voice dropped by an octave.

"Where are you?" Daron slipped on his discarded boxers, scooped up a pair of jogging pants off the chaise, and pulled them on.

"I keep moving," came the quick reply. "Levi has eyes all over Morgan Park."

"Can you make it to the kickback?" Daron asked. Kickback was the code word they used to refer to the house where he conducted the enrichment program. He selected this property because the boys could easily cut through the alley, enter the back gate to get to the side door and into the basement where they had the sessions, all without being seen.

"Yeah."

"I'll meet you there. The door will be unlocked so you can go straight in." With his hand, Daron used the edge of the mattress to guide him closer to the door so he wouldn't disturb the woman he was dating. The glow from his phone helped him find the knob and he entered the hall.

The light came on immediately.

"What's going on?" Cameron asked, making him pause.

Daron slipped the cell in his pocket and glanced over his shoulder into the room. Although she just woke, Cameron's hazel eyes were alert as she swept several strands of dark-brown hair behind her ear. "Amarion has a situation."

"Do you need back up?" she asked, pulling the gown she wore over her head, exposing a pair of breasts so lush Daron wished he could return to bed.

Her kind of backup could leave a higher body count when Chicago was already having issues on that score.

"No." Daron retrieved a t-shirt and grabbed a pair of gym shoes. "I need to get him off the streets and find out what's going on."

Cameron skewered him with an intense stare while he finished dressing before saying, "Call if you need me."

Daron gave her a mock glare and peck before going into his office, quickly gathering a few items, then racing out the door.

His tablet beeped the moment he slid behind the wheel of the Jaguar XJ. On the screen, he watched Amarion approaching the side door of the property. He keyed in the command to disengage the alarms and the locks, allowing the young man to slide into the house.

Daron made the three-minute drive and pulled into the garage of the small two-story brick house. Checking the feed of the security cameras and the drones he had hovering near the property, he made sure no one was walking by or near a window. He slipped from the garage into the house, guided by the dim lighting.

Amarion wore a thin black jacket with a hood and dark-blue jeans. He paced the basement like an expectant father outside the delivery room. "What happened?" Daron asked.

"Remember that story about the girl who went missing but was found with a tracker?" Amarion shifted a small bag from his back and placed it on one of the desks the young men used during sessions.

"You mean Tracy Johnson?" Daron asked, resetting the perimeter alarms. He developed an earring tracking system, to help combat sex trafficking problems and protect young women. Women that tend to be alone a lot either because they lived in a single parent household like Tracy or single women that traveled alone more often than not. For the safety of his clients still utilizing the earrings, Daron created a decoy tracking device for Tracy's mother, Katara, when she went missing.

"Yeah." Amarion swept the hood from his head. His golden-brown face was flushed as he stuffed both hands in his jacket pockets. "Well, Levi wanted that keychain tracker her mom was talking about on the news."

Daron lowered the basement window shutters in order to turn the lights up a few notches. From the outside, no one would notice the difference. "What does this have to do with seeing him murder someone?"

"I'm getting to that." Amarion stopped pacing, pulled out one of the chairs and lowered himself onto the seat. "He arranged for me to snatch the keychain when the mom showed it to the police officer."

"You committed a crime in the police station?" Daron braced himself, unable to believe what he was hearing. He moved in closer. "Amarion, are you serious?"

"That's not the point." Amarion glanced up as Daron hovered next to him. Not an ounce of fear flashed in the boy's dark-brown eyes.

"Let's back up. *Why* does he want the tracker?" Daron had created a fail-safe tool. If anyone attempted to open it, trying to duplicate the technology, the device would short circuit and burn out.

"According to what I heard, he wanted to see if it was emitting any frequency or something like that." Amarion grimaced and shrugged.

"What does that have to do with the shooting and the other witness that may have seen you?" Daron sent Steve, his right-hand man, a text with Levi's name. Over the years, Steve had been the person he trusted with security and to gather intel. By the time they were scheduled to meet later that day, Daron would know everything there was to know about Levi.

"I was there to deliver the device and I hesitated because I recognized the address. Reese and I had been checking out the place for another job for Marquise."

"*Marquise*? What on earth did he have you do?"

"I work for Marquise but he occasionally has me do jobs for Levi." Amarion ran a hand over his curly mohawk, then began fidgeting with his phone. "Maybe five minutes after I put the key chain where they told me, I heard voices arguing. Then Levi was like, 'I don't let anyone mess with my money,' and he shot a man."

"Where was the other witness?" Daron walked toward the big desk at the front of the room.

"Midas was sneaking up to the crafting area from the back at that exact moment." Amarion stood, fiddling with his bag before sliding it onto his back. "He may have seen me when he tried to hide before Levi came round the corner."

"I have to get you out of town for a minute." Daron sent another message to Steve.

Amarion frowned as if Daron said something outrageous. "I can't leave my mom here to catch the heat for me."

"I'll make sure your mother is protected."

"No, sir," he shot back. "That's my job. I'll ride this out for another two weeks until she moves to be with my grandmother." Amarion left the seat, crossed the basement and came closer to Daron. "Mr. Dee, that isn't the real problem."

Daron leaned on the wood desk. "Then what is?"

"I also overheard Levi talking about this new guy who was causing him to lose a lot of money," Amarion whispered, as if they weren't alone in the basement.

"And how's that your problem?" Daron felt he was missing essential information. Maybe it was the "we're" in trouble part. He was waiting to see how Reese—another thief in his program, who specialized in stealing art, played into the scenario.

"He was talking about you."

Daron snapped back to the present. "Are you sure?" Even though he recognized the name from somewhere, Daron couldn't recall ever crossing paths with a Levi Diesel.

Amarion's cell vibrated. His eyes went wide as he checked the message, then flipped the cell to face Daron. "We've just been given an assignment to break into Crossroads Security."

Daron blanched at the mention of his company's name. Why in the hell does Levi have a problem with me? He has to be crazy if he thinks he'll be able to waltz in and take my emergency tracking device.

Daron was certain he needed to put a rush on Steve's efforts to find information because it was clear Levi would be a problem. Daron now understood the "we" Amarion was referring to was him and Amarion.

"Mr. Dee, how are we going to keep Levi from murdering you?"

CHAPTER 2

The early morning activity had Daron on a fifth cup of coffee. He'd left Amarion at the kickback until he had a chance to talk with Reese Pendleton, who wasn't a morning person. Once Reese confirmed there were no whispers of Amarion's name in the streets, he slipped out and Daron set a plan in motion to protect the young man's family. Daron would not have Amarion or his mother's death on his conscience.

When Daron promised Cameron he'd open a legitimate firm that provided security systems, he meant every word. For the last few years, Daron, under the street moniker, The Warden, was the brains behind an illegal organization that helped the FBI takedown Chase Prescott's family business from the inside. Prescott was one of Chicago's most wanted criminals.

He had made a promise that the "cloak and dagger" lifestyle wouldn't shadow them. That was fast becoming a promise he couldn't keep. Especially with Levi gunning for the tracking device housed in a pair of diamond studs—one of the items he had developed as a personal security gadget for single ladies. Not to mention The Castle, which was where wealthy people indulged in any and everything their hearts desired. Daron now handled their security and had taken a seat on the board of directors, which pitted him against powerful criminals.

Steve Beck's call came through as Daron moved the conference pad into position. The holographic image of Steve sitting in a maroon chair appeared in the workspace. "So, Levi Diesel is nothing nice. On paper, it looks like he cleaned up his life and turned it around, but ..."

"It's all for show, I take it." Daron's laptop pinged.

Steve plucked a tablet off a small wooden table next to him. "I didn't have to dig far to uncover dirt on him."

Most times, Steve was well aware that the channels to search for individuals like Cameron, who had a colorful and well-hidden past, took more effort. Most people didn't know she was an expert in breaking the same laws the men in her family were sworn to uphold and protect. Cameron had only recently given up living a double life.

"He sold drugs," Steve added, "had a prostitution ring, an armed robbery crew and this list goes on—all before he turned twenty-one."

"I'm assuming that was the age he "cleaned up" his appearance?"

"Yes. Now he owns a restaurant in Morgan Park and a couple of stores in Chatham and Hyde Park." Steve shifted, typed in some info that populated in the message box on Daron's screen.

"As you now know, he's after my best work."

"You mean to date, right?"

To decrease media attention, Daron had created a decoy tracker for Katara to show the world, instead of revealing the real device that assisted in locating Tracy. Secrecy was the key.

Daron designed the earrings so that all a woman had to do was press it to alert her listed contacts and activate the tracking system. Unfortunately, the more he sold the device to what he thought were good women with high-risk factors, the more chances of the word getting out. If traffickers were in the know, they would make sure the earrings were off before moving their victims. The few clients he'd sold the tracker to were still wearing them, which made the decoy necessary.

"The team is fully aware, even though breaking into the satellite office won't do him any good." Steve placed the tablet next to the laptop on a nearby table. "We don't store equipment there."

Reese and Amarion already knew that because that's how they met him. They had attempted to break into Crossroads Security office and searched the place, unaware he'd taken down the alarm system to let them in. After Daron made his presence known, he had a long conversation with them about choices and consequences. The fact that Amarion had come to him showed he was committed to his new path. Unlike his aunt, who was still attracted to that fast money lifestyle.

"Contact Red to see if he'd be willing to fly in from New York and discreetly find Midas," Daron said. Red was a man who went on an undercover black ops assignment, got burned, and ended up working with Bishop. Daron never quite got the full story of how that came to be, especially since he never really stopped helping law enforcement catch the bad guys.

"I'll reach out to him," Steve replied, typing into his cell. "I'll have him send you an audio recording of the conversation."

"Is my aunt staying out of trouble?" Daron wished he could convince Brandi that no one had tampered with his brother's car. Despite every attempt, she was still convinced he'd been murdered. Unfortunately, Brandi couldn't know that Troy was alive and in witness protection.

Steve leaned forward, resting an elbow on each thigh, looking more like a high school grad than the director and part-owner of Crossroads Security. "She rolls with a hard-core group of friends but she hasn't gotten in any trouble yet."

"Give me the rundown on Marquise's involvement with The Castle." Daron settled onto a stool in front of the long rectangle workbench.

He hadn't been able to wrap his mind around Khalil selecting him as one of the people to help turn things around. Of course, his son, Vikkas, was an obvious choice. The others had attended Macro International Magnet School where Khalil had mentored the majority of them. Daron had met all of the criteria and was selected to attend but had declined since he wanted the program that allowed him to take classes at a local university.

"Oh, before we get to that, I've assigned a team to Calvin. Mia is officially on the payroll."

Calvin Atwood had created a spectacular invention, which made the wearer practically invisible to the naked eye by reflecting the images around it. The device became such a coveted item that several governments had sent teams to kill him, simply to make off with the project for their own purposes. Daron was working with him to install trackers in the device. Mia Jakob was now his fiancée, but she came by way of an agency hired to protect him and the invention.

Now that he and Calvin had teamed up, Marquise was determined to make problems for the project unless Daron cooperated with his demands. And that wasn't going to happen.

CHAPTER 3

Daron hated that he'd brought an additional threat to an already dangerous project. However, when he agreed to participate, he had no idea he'd become a King of The Castle.

"How did the meetings go at The Castle?" Steve asked, as he pulled up an image of Khalil sporting shiny black hair with a sliver of grey. His deep-olive skin looked vibrant, unlike the pale tone he had acquired after a failed attempt to murder him the day Daron visited him in the hospital several weeks ago.

"Interesting." Daron spread his fingertips and opened a folder on The Castle onscreen. The hospital visit had a profound effect.

The edge of Khalil's mouth curled up ever so slightly as the medical equipment hummed and beeped in the background. "The program that paid for your college tuition and allowed you to start your business right after high school was a Castle initiative."

Daron slid back in the seat and silently cursed. He'd wanted to give back to the program but by his second semester at the university it no longer existed. "You do realize that my membership and being connected to Bishop is going to create issues."

"Bishop has been in your life since you were young, so I know you can handle it." Khalil grimaced as if speaking was painful. That didn't stop him from talking about the criminal mastermind who had left Daron The Castle membership. "You're needed on this team, in this brotherhood. More importantly, the next young person with a brilliant mind and a talent like yours will need people who think outside of the box to teach them how to create wealth and provide substance to others."

Daron pondered those words for a moment.

"I'm already working on something. A large group would slow down the process of moving from concept to reality." Daron was happy for the first time in years. No amount of wealth could buy that. He'd just spent the last five years being a sacrificial lamb for others. The people who benefited the most seemed to be the biggest "gangs" around—the CIA, FBI, and Interpol. The things some of them did behind the scenes ranked them right up there with the criminals. Putting his happiness and well-being on the back burner had become taxing. He didn't know if he was willing to do it again, especially so soon after he had finally managed to get back to doing what he loved full time. Now he had someone who didn't need him to complete her, and having a family was once again a possibility. "I'll consider it, but there's a great personal risk to take this one on. Even if I agree, I'm not promising long term."

"I'll take what I can get." Khalil reached for Daron's hand the minute he vacated the chair at his bedside, his slight moan indicating that the pain meds were wearing off. "Who is she?"

The image of Cameron's hazel eyes, deep dimples and full lips came to mind. "A woman who'll dive into the depths of hell for someone she loves, and uses that same amount of energy to destroy people who make her an enemy."

Khalil closed his eyes momentarily, inhaling and exhaling as if trying to steady himself. "Participating shouldn't make her an enemy."

"No, it shouldn't, but keeping secrets that involve proximity to the type of criminals who've been managing The Castle will not keep her in my life."

"Daron. Daron." Steve called out, snapping Daron out of his reflection.

"So the meetings changed your stance on getting involved?"

"At first, I felt it wasn't my fight." He wanted to be an inactive member but he could hear his mother saying, *making no decision is a decision.* "The director of the agency, who was vetting membership, waited until Khalil was on a five-year world tour to become lax on the strict criteria which governed The Castle, allowing criminals to buy a seat at the table and pushing out any dissenters."

The Castle members with the biggest stake had a say in the general running of the property, which led to Khalil's current problem. The majority of those members were now criminals who had moved away from Khalil's original vision. Daron had already been threatened by Marquise Sinclair, a crime boss over an international art theft ring, who had become a member of The Castle for the power and the network to back up his schemes.

"It's an ugly situation." Steve grabbed a small black remote from the table.

"We need to figure out how the shooters got past their state-of-the-art security." Daron pulled out the top drawer of his work station and retrieved a laptop. "And it might give Dro a clue and some insight on who hired them."

Grant Khambrel's image popped up next to Steve. He ran a premier commercial construction company in Texas; was a self-made multimillionaire and his company had been selected to renovate the United Center. Daron, who had also signed his acceptance on the same day as Grant, hadn't expected him to be on the list.

"According to the whispers in the streets, people were waiting eagerly for his arrival in Chicago. They weren't the good kind of people, either." Steve frowned, indicating there was much more to the story.

The laptop pinged. Daron checked the message from Steve, reading the details surrounding the rumor on how Grant started in the business. "Damn, that's not good."

"And before you ask, the info is from a reliable source, but it's still only a rumor."

Grant's image disappeared, replaced by the person Daron knew would make the cut. Kaleb Valentine, a real estate developer in the Metro Detroit area and former gang member who turned State's evidence against a well-known gang leader.

"The property he recently acquired on the South Side of Chicago burned down. Five people were trapped inside." Steve pulled up the photos from the scene. "It's a very active investigation."

Daron's laptop chimed as another message came through.

Steve stood, his top half nearly disappearing from view. "Last person."

Next Jaidev Maharaj's face appeared. "He runs the Chetan Health Center. Seems he's under industry scrutiny for incorporating unconventional methods and one of his comatose patients is nearly eight months pregnant."

"I don't understand the issue."

"Eight months pregnant," Steve repeated. "She's been a guest of the facility for a year."

"Well damn, that has to be eating him up." Daron figured him to be a man who took immense pride in what he did and cared deeply about the people. "How could that happen?"

"The police are investigating him and his male employees. The State is trying to close his facility down—permanently."

Daron added some notes about a device that could prevent another patient from having a similar experience in the future.

"While Shastra, Mariano, Victor, and Dwayne didn't produce anything that screamed immediate concern, remember this was an initial search." Steve lowered himself back onto the chair and tapped a few keys.

Steve was referring to Shastra "Shaz" Bostwick, an immigration lawyer who serviced a wide range of clients that came to America from all over the world. Mariano "Reno" DeLuca had amassed several properties in the Chatham area and opened a women's shelter. Victor Alejandro "Dro" Reyes, who owned a Crisis Management Company, was better known in the streets as a fixer; someone who discreetly cleaned up and handled "situations" for high profile people. Dwayne Harper was a local college professor teaching world studies. They had to practically twist his arm to get him to agree to become involved in The Castle.

"And you can include Vik in that grouping." Vikkas Germaine was Khalil's son as well as an international and intellectual property lawyer. "It'll be interesting to see if Jai and Vikkas will bump heads a lot. They could actually be twins." He pulled up the drone feed from The Castle before sending it to Steve.

"Why is that?"

"Just a feeling I have." Considering the group of men Khalil put together, Daron knew decision-making time was going to be interesting. Vikkas had taken the lead in both meetings, but he doubted that would always be the case in the future.

"I've put Linc on security for Calvin's shipment since Nicco is Khalil's main protector."

Daron shifted the ghost drone, at least that's what Cameron called it. He managed to make it invisible to the naked eye, all except several small internal pieces. "The shipment should arrive soon so that we can dive in."

"Time's up. We have a lot on our plate." Steve glanced at the Rolex on his dark brown wrist. "I'll get you a picture of Levi ASAP."

"What about the candidates to manage my program?"

"A preliminary report should be finished soon." Steve rose, walking toward the center of the screen. "You're sure you don't want a protection team?"

"Positive."

Having a security detail the last few years was necessary. Now that he has been without any for a while, he wasn't ready to go back to being accompanied everywhere.

"Try not to get yourself killed," Steve warned.

Unfortunately, if Cameron found out about The Castle, she'd be the first one to do the honors.

CHAPTER 4

The perimeter alarm beeped moments after Daron ended the call. He immediately grabbed his weapon, then snatched up a tablet from the counter. He glanced at the display screen and sighed, putting the Beretta back in place as he chuckled.

Cameron Stone kept him on his toes. She loved to test his security system for any weakness. Last week, she found and used a sensor that had been blocked by a branch to enter the property undetected, but he'd already installed a secondary one. Today, she managed to bypass the first two but wasn't aware of the third one. Daron didn't know if her actions were meant to keep him sharp or to make sure her skills stayed on point. Maybe a little of both.

He made his way from the basement workshop up the stairs to greet her. When she approached, he pulled open a steel door camouflaged by a layer of Cherrywood.

"Hey gorgeous." Daron stared at her baggy workout pants and over-sized shirt. Not that she didn't look beautiful, but he couldn't wait until she changed into the clothing that accentuated her shape, and rocked those high heels he loved. His mind flashed back to the evening at the garage when she was ready to rumble with Marquise's men, wearing one of his preferred outfits. Intense anger filled him as he thought how the incident ruined the remainder of his night.

She gave him a peck on the lips before sliding past him. "What's that face for? Did one of your top candidates for the program get eliminated?" She slipped off her sneakers as he locked up. "Warden."

Daron smiled, realizing he'd taken too long to respond but not missing the intentional use of the name associated with his illegal past. "Not yet."

"Mmm." Cameron's eyes seemed to study his face again as she slung the backpack strap onto one shoulder. "Are we still meeting up with Calvin and Mia?"

"They rescheduled, but we're leaving within the hour for our dinner date."

"I'm good with that." A slight smile curved her lips, then her expression darkened. "Should I come prepared?"

He stared into her eyes, hating the brown contacts covering the natural hazel color and her face altered to hide those adorable dimples. A reminder that, once again she was hiding in plain sight. "To have a good time?" he hedged.

"That's not what I'm talking about." She lifted an eyebrow but didn't say anything else.

Unfortunately, having developed a tracker that located a missing girl, working with Calvin on an invention worth billions, and taking a seat on The Castle's board of directors didn't bode well for Daron remaining under the radar. "Did anything else unusual happen besides your mom showing up?"

"You don't have to avoid my question." She stepped into his path as he made his way to the basement. He felt the heat of her gaze lasered on him. "We're a team, remember."

"Yes, and we live a life where we always need to be ready for anything." Daron kissed her forehead then turned her in the direction of the master bedroom.

Drawing attention to himself had also put a spotlight on her. When he met her under the alias of Tandria Jenkins, her hazel eyes were always on display, as well as her reddish-brown hair that skimmed the middle of her back. Now the hair was black and hidden under a sable wig unless they were at his home and staying in all night.

"For a while, we weren't," Cameron pointed out in a solemn tone. "Not like this."

His heart ached because their post-retirement bliss hadn't lasted longer. Things hadn't been the same since the day Tracy went missing and all the madness started. "Babe, take your shower." He patted her round ass. Daron wished the answer could be different but until he was no longer working with Calvin, The Castle, and now the program, he was always expecting trouble. "I'll be in my workshop."

"I hope you picked a good restaurant for tonight," Cameron said as she walked away.

Forty-five minutes later, Daron glanced back as Cameron quietly slid into the workroom wearing a peach spaghetti-strap dress that hugged her curves, eliciting some carnal and sensual thoughts. Daron smiled as her arms wrapped around his waist. Her breasts pressed against him as she placed her chin over his shoulder, giving him a squeeze.

"What are you working on?"

"A tattoo, in case a man doesn't wear an earring." Daron couldn't say it was for Dro because Cameron knew nothing of The Castle or the eight men he was working with. "It would work similarly to the earring but it pulses if you accidentally activate the sensor."

She picked up the schematics and the circuitry the tattoos required. "Where will the tattoo be worn?"

"On the inside of the wrist." Daron admired the lion, with flames as the mane, centered inside three circles. Between the last two circles were nine spearheads. Simple yet stunning. "JD drew it for me."

"Nice. I'll give my cousin a hard time about that later since he claims he's too busy to do anything for me." She lowered herself onto a seat, then put the items back. "You need to rethink a couple of things. Maybe have a way it can be turned off and quickly turned back on in case of emergency."

"Why? When it pulses, the person would just turn it off." Daron flipped his wrist up to show the one he'd been testing.

"Because if I'm feeling frisky, push you onto a bed and hold you down by the wrist." Cameron stood and grabbed his wrist, pinning it against the countertop.

The pulse was immediate and not only on his wrist.

She lowered those luscious lips to his, her tongue exploring the inside of his mouth. Her body skimmed his, electrifying his senses. Daron slid his free hand over her round ass, deepening the kiss. He pulled her into his chest as she attempted to move away. With one arm, he cleared some space before lifting her onto the tabletop. The cell's alarm blared, reminding him it was time for them to leave.

She chuckled, her lips curled into a mischievous grin. "See, this time I don't think your mind was on your tracker."

Daron rested his forehead on hers. "Point taken."

* * *

Forty minutes later, Daron and Cameron were at Mastro's Steakhouse in the heart of Chicago sipping whiskey mules and waiting for the arrival of a Porterhouse steak and Lobster Tails. His cell chimed with an image of Levi. The picture was of a man no darker than a piece of toffee with piercing eyes and a nick in the left eyebrow. The same man who was across the room staring at him. The tattoos on both his arms peeked out from under the cuff of the crisp white shirt he wore.

"What's wrong?" Cameron discreetly glanced over her shoulder.

"It seems I have a new admirer." Daron watched as a muscular man, draped in an expensive light-blue suit, rose to his full six feet as two men at the tables near him did the same.

Levi motioned to his men to remain seated as he made his way to Daron's table.

"Daron Kincaid, I'm Levi Diesel. I've seen you around the Morgan Park area," Levi lied without missing a beat. "I thought I'd introduce myself."

Daron shook the extended hand noticing the robot mechanism tattoo on the back of it and didn't miss the way Levi angled his body to reveal the weapon under his jacket.

"Is this beautiful woman your wife?" Levi focused on Cameron with lust instantly flaring in his eyes. "I see we can't be business partners because I already know I want what you have."

Levi lifted Cameron's hand from the table toward his mouth. Before it made contact, she snatched her hand back, giving an evil sneer that only seemed to draw Levi in more. "Dude, I don't think so." Cameron shot him an evil glare. "I only hang with men who have decorum, that was a classless move right there."

Levi's demeanor shifted from charming to combative.

"It's time for you to return to your table." Daron stood, towering over the man by three inches.

Levi leaned toward Daron and whispered, "Be prepared to lose everything." He smiled, focusing on Cameron, who didn't look away. "Pleasure meeting you, gorgeous."

CHAPTER 5

The last few weeks reminded Cameron exactly how fragile her world was. Saving a missing girl had been the first domino to fall. More had gone down since then. The Levi situation led to an argument about the garage incident. Daron had tried to send her to the car while he handled the three men who followed them from the restaurant into the parking structure.

Daron is no longer acting like a retired man.

His body language had been off, more like The Warden. While he'd been honest about the Levi character, up until then, Daron had been side-stepping questions and was vague about even the simple things. Something big was going on. She could feel it in her bones.

After taking off the wig and the brown contacts in Daron's master bathroom, she padded barefoot into the living room and joined him on a black leather couch.

"What was in Bishop's envelope?" Cameron asked snapping a picture of Daron as he slipped off his tie, not only because he looked devastatingly handsome but because she felt the need to capture an image of this version of him before he completely reverted to being The Warden. All signs pointed to that possibility.

"I haven't read it." He unleashed a sexy grin as he loosened several shirt buttons, opening them to reveal his muscular frame. "After the file he left me spoke to your positive achievements, I figured the letter was to let me know who you were."

Cameron mulled that over a moment. "Why would he give you the letter?" She placed her cell on the ottoman next to the remote.

"Bishop's my godfather," Daron admitted, staring at her intensely as though trying to gauge her reaction to that piece of news.

"Whoa." She was floored but now everything made sense. "When were you going to tell me that tidbit of information?"

"I figured it would come up naturally as we got to know each other." Daron shrugged off his jacket, laying it over the arm of the couch. His cell chimed and he glanced at the display, quickly silencing the sound.

Cameron stared at him without hiding her displeasure. She couldn't believe he waited until now to reveal something that important and that she had to prod him into doing so. "What other information are you keeping from me?"

"Probably the same amount as you, Babe." Daron smiled and shot her a "get over it" glare. "Even if we did a data dump of our history right now, we'd probably still forget to tell each other something."

She wanted to disagree but he had a point. "When you open the letter, I'd like to know the contents."

Daron shifted his gaze to her with one raised eyebrow. "Is there something specific *you* think's in there? I can get it from the safe now."

She placed a hand on his thigh as he attempted to move away, then shook her head. "In the last few years, Bishop had the team working more jobs at once. Almost as if he was trying to keep us distracted."

Daron reclaimed his space and his hold on her. "Finding out he had an incurable disease probably upped the ante for him."

She stiffened at the mention of her criminal mastermind boss's fatal condition.

As he shifted to place an arm over the back of the couch, Daron's gaze seared into her. "Maybe he was tying up loose ends and getting things done that he'd put off for too long."

"Maybe, but nothing's ever that simple when it comes to Bishop." Cameron had been spending so much time getting her new gym facility up and running and hanging out with Daron, she hadn't handled the file Bishop had left her.

Cameron wished their connection was purely sexual, but Daron Kincaid had a hold on her heart. She snuggled into his side and didn't miss his derisive glance at her feet before he pretended to check the button on the television remote. Normally the high heels stayed on her feet until Daron removed them but the disagreement changed all of that.

Daron selected a channel, dropped the remote next to him, grabbed her legs and situated them in his lap. He slowly stroked her legs, causing ripples of desire to shoot through her body. Evidently, Daron had already moved past their earlier tiff. He picked up the two containers with cake they grabbed from a bakery on the way home, handing her one with a fork. "Have you figured out what's going on with your dad?"

Cameron looked up at him, wondering at the shift in conversation. "Trenton's been following Jake. He's visiting a lot of doctors' offices. Sometimes he seems to have an appointment. Other times, he seems to follow them."

"Is it possible that he doesn't want to go under their care until he's sure they have no connection to any of his old cases?" He moved his lemon cake to the side and slid a fork into her amaretto dessert.

"While I was at my mom's, I snuck into his office," Cameron took a few bites before he thought she didn't want it at all. His sweet tooth was legendary. "I managed to find a list of doctors in a file he had in the hidden compartment in his desk. There are doctors from New York and the DC area as well." She hadn't had time to get into his locked cabinet before hearing her mom forced her to race back to the living room. That way, the petite woman didn't have to pretend not to know Cameron was snooping.

"Could this be connected to one of your brothers' cases?" Daron asked, switching out her empty container for the remainder of the lemon cake.

"I can't find that out without having Trent do some hacking." She wouldn't ask that of him unless she thought it was unavoidable.

Daron kissed her neck, causing her breath to quicken. "If you need me to, I can call in some favors that don't require him to come out of retirement."

"I'll keep that in mind." Cameron shifted playfully, blocking his fork as he went for a piece of cake. He always had a voracious appetite for food, life and her. "We'll follow him a little while longer. Trenton was compiling a list of facts to help figure out the common factor that could give me a clue what Jake is into."

"Did I tell you how beautiful you looked tonight?" Daron cupped his hand around her ass and shifted her on his lap.

"Maybe once or twice." She slipped an arm around his neck.

Daron's finger traced the curve of her breast while he leaned in to deliver a sensual and steamy kiss. His left hand slipped over the top of her legs, then rested on the side of her thighs. Every nerve in her body tingled with excitement. Daron's hand slid under her dress, cupping her bare behind before traveling up her back and pulling down the zipper.

She slipped her arms out the straps of the dress as his touch increased the throbbing need building inside her.

Daron cupped her breasts, lowering his mouth and swirling his tongue around each nipple.

Cameron situated herself on his lap and slowly rocked her hips against his growing erection as she unbuttoned his shirt. She braced herself on his knees then arched and rolled her hips as he alternated between massaging one breast as he sucked and nibbled at the other.

"Damn, Cam." He brought his lips to hers.

Placing both hands on his shoulders, she removed his shirt. Her fingers traced the muscles as he worked to erase any lingering thoughts about their earlier disagreement. They would address it some other time. Daron shifted and laid her on the couch.

"I'm a very lucky man," Daron said in a voice that was deep and low as he tugged the dress completely off.

"That you are," she replied in a seductive tone as her eyes wandered over his sculpted body.

His lips made a trail from the inner ankle, up the calf to the thigh. Each kiss sent tingling sensations shooting through her body. Cameron's breath caught as his mouth hovered over her throbbing center, teasing her with a flick of the tongue then moving to the other leg.

She gently guided him back between her thighs, feeling the heat of his breath as he chuckled.

"Is there something that you want, Beautiful?" Daron taunted. His tongue twirled and danced over the bundle of nerves at her core, which made it difficult to speak.

"That," she managed to say as he slid a thigh over one shoulder. Daron's masterful tongue awakened a ravenous desire that had her grinding into him until her entire body quivered.

His long, tapered fingers slid into her center as his lips blazed a path up her torso. He pinched, sucked and teased her breasts as his strokes left her breathless and shaking uncontrollably.

He unbuttoned his slacks letting them and the boxers fall away, then sheathed himself and entered her in one powerful thrust. "What do you want tonight?" His rhythm remained steady. "Slow and gentle or fast and hard?"

"Fast and hard," she replied.

Daron gripped her behind and pounded into her like a man who just ended a thirty-year vow of celibacy.

"Yes." Cameron lifted her hips to meet each stroke.

He pulled out, easily maneuvered her to both knees as if they were in a bed and not on a couch. Her breasts bounced as he impaled her from behind. She slammed her ass into him, bracing herself on the arm of the couch, barely keeping her left leg on the cushion. His name slipped from her lips repeatedly as his smooth, quick powerful strokes brought that electrifying ecstasy which kept her craving him constantly.

"It's time for you to get what you want." In one swift motion, Daron lifted her and positioned her to straddle him backward. He squeezed her bosom as she rode him hard.

Cameron couldn't see Daron's face but felt the tremors in his hands every once in a while, as they roamed her body. When his fingers glided over her thighs and stroked her center, the only one trembling was her.

Daron held her close, sliding a hand in her long hair, kissing her neck and gently massaging her breast. "Now, are you ready to give me slow and sweet?"

Cameron recovered then straddled him once again, sliding both arms around his neck. "Let's do this." She slowly lifted up then slammed down, rolling her hips and making her breasts brush against his chest before repeating the process then lowering her lips to his.

"Yes." His voice was breathy.

She lowered her lips to his, exploring, tasting, and enjoying the sight of his eyes rolling when she made certain moves.

"Let's take this to the bedroom," Daron said, as he lifted her from the couch.

Cameron wrapped her legs around his waist, returning her lips to his. He made it as far the wall near the door before he pinned her against it, taking her with a fiery voracity that left them soaked in bliss and barely standing.

She could feel his heart hammering against her chest. They remained there until the rapid breathing in her ears slowed and her body stopped trembling against his.

Daron carried her to the bed where they began a slow and intense mind-blowing exploration of each other's body until they had nothing left to give.

CHAPTER 6

Daron fumed as he read a text from Cameron stating Levi made an unwanted appearance at her self-defense class. He quickly replied to the message. BABE BE CAREFUL. HE'S A DANGEROUS MAN.

While he wasn't happy about Levi stalking his woman, at least he could warn and talk to her about it, unlike the situation with Marquise. Daron had to make time to visit and figure out who brought down the Castle's security system.

"Our first group of young men are almost out the door," Pedro Garcia stated. The psychologist and educational specialist powered on a laptop before glancing at Daron for a reaction.

Daron hoped Levi wouldn't discover that Amarion had witnessed the murder before Pedro could finalize all the arrangements to get him set up and his mother safely settled with the grandmother. "We gave them the tools to change but their resolve is already being tested. They have to really want it."

The conversation made Daron think of the audio file Red sent over. He slid in a pair of earbuds then pulled it up to listen while he and Pedro waited in the basement of the kickback house for the young men to arrive. The recording began to play as he reviewed the work schedule Calvin emailed to make sure he didn't have any conflicts.

"Midas," Red said in a low but clear voice. "I have a mutual interest in knowing whether Levi is aware that you were in the room when he killed that man."

"That little kid is out here being a snitch," Midas growled.

Dammit. Daron was hoping Midas hadn't seen Amarion.

"No," Red quickly supplied. "I'm here to make sure Levi never knows that either of you were in the room."

"As long as the kid keeps his mouth shut, you ain't got to worry about me." Midas paused then said, "I got my hands full trying to make sure I don't end up like my partner."

"I have an associate looking to shut Levi down, so if you get any information that can do that, give this number a call."

The alarm sensors beeped and Daron pressed stop and took out the earbuds, grateful that he had confirmation Levi was unaware Amarion was in the building at the time of the murder. He peered at the tablet to confirm the identities of the young men, who were various hues of brown but every bit African-American, before unlocking the doors.

Reese and Amarion walked in together laughing and talking with Cedric trailing behind them. Cedric, a hacker with the potential to earn a living developing games or creating the next big social media platform instead of taking jobs off the dark web, quietly entered the room slowing when he reached Daron.

"Whazzup, Mr. Dee," Amarion asked as Reese gave him a slight nod.

"Teach," Reese said, putting more of his focus on Pedro.

"I'm not like them," Cedric whispered, pulling out a laptop. "They're charismatic handsome go-getters. I'm a loner who sits behind a computer."

Daron wondered where that comment came from or what had happened to cause him to make this statement. Maybe the thought of making the next big step had startled him into playing the comparison game. "You wouldn't have been selected if we didn't think you had potential to do great things. But you have to fight for a different life," Daron replied. Constantly questioning his worth would get Cedric in trouble and keep him on the wrong side of the law. He was the only one who didn't have anyone dishing out assignments or consequences for not completing them.

"Okay." Cedric went back to his area in the corner of the basement near the stairs, but his demeanor stated he wasn't convinced yet.

Daron and Pedro's presence in the room was mainly for support. The initial week was when they did the evaluations using the individual plans Pedro developed for each of them. For the next hour, Pedro and Daron reviewed the preliminary data Steve had sent on the candidates for director to oversee expanding the enrichment program while occasionally answering questions from the young men.

Several phones chimed as a reminder that the session had ended. The young men hurriedly gathered their belongings and prepared to leave.

"Hey, before you go, I want to say I'm proud of you," Daron announced, which stopped their movements. "It's not easy to decide to change your life and then take the steps to make it happen."

"Yo, Mr. Dee don't tell us you're about to get mushy on us," Reese teased, as he brushed his fade then checked his image in his cell.

Daron chuckled at his antics. The boy was a little vain. "No. I'm reminding you not to be limited by someone else's definition of success and don't be afraid to adjust your path to find your own happiness."

"It won't be easy," Pedro chimed in, coming from behind the desk and standing near the group. "Know that you'll make mistakes, as well as bad decisions."

"Own them and do better." Daron stared at the young men, silently praying for their strength, wisdom, and ability to endure. "Just try not to do anything that's hard to bounce back from."

Amarion lowered himself on to a chair while the other two leaned on the desks.

"People with amazing talent have not excelled because they didn't recover from the damage incurred from the first major set-back," Pedro added.

Daron knew he needed to wrap it up. Reese was checking his phone again and Cedric was fiddling with his bag. "Be prepared for life to challenge your decisions." He glanced at Amarion, then collected his tablet, signaling to the group he was done.

"We have something we want you to consider." Pedro tapped his inner wrist where he'd been testing a tattoo for Daron.

Daron retrieved a set of tattoo trackers from a manila envelope on the desk. "We have a way for you to contact us in an emergency if you're unable to call."

Amarion's shoulders dropped as though he was relieved.

"You have the choice to take it or not, but we're trusting you not to tell anyone this technology exists," Pedro added.

"One thing we're good at is keeping our mouths shut." Reese looked back at the other two and they nodded.

"Three quick taps against a hard surface and holding for a few seconds will turn it on and alert us you're in trouble." Daron then explained how to attach the tattoo and answered questions.

The tattoos could stay on a month without any maintenance through most conditions. His fingers were crossed that he'd be taking them back and sending the boys off to their new cities and their new lives. Over the next two weeks, Daron needed them not to get into the kind of trouble that could put a stop to their plans.

The young men each picked a style of tattoo and Daron registered them into his system.

"On that note, let's get you moving so you won't need to use these tonight." Pedro glanced at his watch. "I'll see you next time."

Reese and Cedric bounced up the stairs.

"Mr. Dee. You may want to dump your ride for a while." Amarion spoke softly, watching the stairs. To make sure the other two had cleared the space. "Levi has people searching for your car."

"Thanks for the heads up."

Amarion nodded. Reese tipped back down just as Amarion headed up the stairs causing Reese to change direction. Daron waited fifteen minutes before he locked up. Watching the drone feeds, he gathered that armed men had checked out the Jag several blocks over. Daron and Pedro exited when he was sure there were no obvious threats on the street. He would get the Porsche Panamera out of storage tomorrow and leave the Jag parked in front so no one could tell when he came and went.

Pedro patted Daron on the shoulder. "Tell Steve thanks for the detail."

Daron nodded, realizing that comment was to let him know that his friend had accepted the offer for protection. A car pulled out shortly after Pedro. The cell vibrated in the pocket of Daron's slacks, then a familiar ring tone filtered into the air. "What's up?"

"Aunt Bee is clowning. I texted the address," Steve huffed.

"I'm on the move." Daron slipped into the Jag, firing up the engine and noticing someone standing across the street on the porch of a house with white siding, staring at the vehicle. The call switched to the Bluetooth. "What did she do?"

The man on the porch pulled out a cell as Daron took off down the block.

"Our man dragged her off some lady but she keeps coming at her like a bulldog. She walked away but he suspects that Brandi will double back as soon as he leaves."

Fifteen minutes later, Daron arrived at a red brick building with a woman sitting on the porch talking to the security guard assigned to Brandi leaned on the rail. His stance bored. He texted the man letting him know he could return to the sedan.

Not five minutes later, the older woman who had been speaking with the guard stepped through the gate heading toward the corner. She sported reddish-orange hair, a pink tank top and too-tight cut out jeans.

Daron scanned the block.

Brandi came up on the woman so fast Daron almost got whiplash.

Man, I didn't know she could still move that fast.

He bolted from the Jag, sprinting in their direction.

Brandi snatched the woman up by her shirt. "Did you work on Troy's car?"

The woman struggled to push Brandi away. "I don't know what you're talking about."

"You can lie to someone who don't know what you do for Roger."

The woman swung on Brandi, whose arm reared back before clocking the lady's jaw with a fist that sported a ring on every finger. Blood splattered from the woman's mouth.

"You two are too old to be brawling like high schoolers." Daron approached, tussling with the women in an attempt to separate them.

Brandi continued swinging. "Stop, Aunt Bee."

"I'm your elder." Brandi turned to Daron getting in his face. "You don't talk to me like that."

"Then act like you've got some sense." He focused on the lady whose crow's feet, dark under-eye bags, and neck wrinkles had her appearing much older than she had looked from a distance. An angry bruise was forming on her jaw. "Go."

In response, the stranger crinkled up her face and lifted one side of her mouth almost as if she was snarling at him. "Huh? This is *my* block. This heifer rolled up, questioning people like she's 5-0 or sumthing."

Brandi's hands balled into fists but Daron managed to hold her back. He glanced at the woman like she was crazy. "You responded as if I asked you a question."

"You act like I should address you as Mr. President," the stranger roared, narrowing her dark-brown eyes as a man in an Adidas jogging suit approached.

"Maybe you should, I've issued my executive order and fully expect it to be followed." Daron scanned the area to find people fumbling with their phones. He pressed a device in his pocket, blocking everyone's ability to record. "I *can* let her go."

The woman snarled something that rhymed with witch then walked away, heading toward a man, whose skin was several shades darker than Daron's pale complexion. He acknowledged her with a nod and kept advancing in Daron's direction.

"Brandi, do I have to get a restraining order on you?" the man asked.

"Do that, Roger." Brandi flicked up a middle finger, causing him to scowl. "Cause I'll tell them about why I'm all up in your face."

Daron realized he'd just been unofficially introduced to the man who Brandi believed killed Troy.

Now he had to find out why.

CHAPTER 7

Maybe Levi was into mind games.

Levi issued a threat and had been relatively quiet, besides having people watch a Jag that hadn't moved in days. Not a good sign. He'd rather have Levi out there making moves he could counter instead of working in silence. Especially when life was pulling Daron in so many different directions. The consequences of dropping the ball on any of his obligations had deadly repercussions. That's why he'd returned to the lavish estate in Wilmette. He needed to assess the security system and figure out who brought down the entire thing, buying time to put multiple bullets in Kahlil and one in Vikkas.

"Since none of the boys in your program sell drugs, I can't figure why Levi feels you're costing him money." Steve jarred Daron back into the conversation they'd been having about Levi.

"Maybe he had a deal with the traffickers to move drugs when they move the girls," Daron suggested, driving through the wooded grounds toward the acres of sprawling greenery.

"We'll figure out what we're missing," Steve assured, but his tone signaled something far from it.

"I don't doubt that. I just don't want that to happen moments before he lays waste to my life."

Daron disconnected the call, sitting in the car taking in the beauty for a second. The Castle property had an eighteen-hole golf course, horse stables, swimming pool, basketball and tennis court, lake, and more features than he cared to list. He launched the ghost drone after exiting the Porsche Panamera and entered the foyer. All anyone could see was the golden elegance and lavish beauty of the space.

"Mr. Kincaid, Mr. Vikkas will be with you in a moment," Terrell announced then returned to his post near the door. Professional. Crisp. Well-groomed and strapped.

The foyer was designed to impress, without safety in mind. Many people saw the area as a magnificent showpiece, but it was a threat zone and security nightmare, a death tunnel. The beautiful floors were not flat. The way the ground shifted reminded Daron of a speed bump. He wondered if it was created to prevent vehicles from crashing through the doors and getting too far down the hall way. A great idea until an active shooter or an emergency evacuation, then it would be a disaster.

Vikkas hadn't given Daron any reason to distrust him but he didn't know enough about the dynamic between father and son. Had Vikkas been jealous of the men his father had mentored? And if Daron's instinct held, he needed to do a little recon on Jai. Something was off and no one else could see it except him.

Daron would have to assess which of the security personnel would stay on and which ones would be let go. "Were you here the morning Khalil was shot?"

"No, sir." Terrell's shoulders stiffened before his hand went up to adjust his earpiece.

Daron created a palm control for the drone. The drone would pick up on things he missed, like Vikkas' facial expression when he thought no one was looking, people quickly stepping in and out of the room, cameras shifting, and guards' reactions.

Vikkas appeared in the foyer.

"I don't understand why my father hired you to handle security." His face was taut with displeasure. "Let alone become a King when you inherited your membership from a criminal."

"Alleged criminal," Daron corrected. The rumors about Bishop didn't do the man justice. "Your displeasure with my presence needs to be taken up with Khalil. Now are you going to allow me to do my job or are you going to continue to bitch and moan about the fact that I'm here?"

"What do you need?" Vikkas' tone was curt. The set of his shoulders indicated Vikkas was far from letting his annoyance go. "Why is this visit necessary, when everything seemed settled the day you placed Nicco with us?"

"I need access to the security system." Daron followed him down the hall. "How did you and your father survive?"

Vikkas' head snapped in Daron's direction. His olive skin was flushed and his eyes conveyed his displeasure. "What?"

"This foyer, unless you're on the second level or near the stairs, doesn't provide anyone with adequate cover." Daron was curious about who was present in the foyer besides the two men. "Was there anything out of place in the foyer that day?"

Vikkas sighed, "When I met my father near the entrance, I realized I'd left my wallet and turned back. I was on my way to retrieve it when a shadow flickered and my father lunged at the shooter." Vikkas touched his arm, the place where the bullet grazed him. "A second intruder rushed me while my father was wrestling with the shooter. He was holding his own. By the time I had my guy down, the trespasser had the upper hand. He fired several shots at my father. The gun jammed. A third person raced in and said they had to go. The two men backed out so quickly. I couldn't stop them."

Daron filtered through the story, searching for inconsistencies. "It was divine intervention that you and Khalil were close to the door. Had you been further back, you would've been dead before either of you had a chance to react." Daron scanned the lengthy golden entrance with three red strips of carpet, two of which went up a double set of stairs and the other down the hallway in the center.

"I need a list of the men working here that day," Daron stated as they neared an entrance.

Vikkas entered a code, pulled the handle and walked into the security room.

I should have known the security room would be a grand affair.

Fourteen flat-screen monitors lined the front wall. Several surveillance desks with leather executive chairs, with four monitors to each desk, lined two of the walls with a large station in the center.

"This is Scott, one of the supervisors." Vikkas gestured to a heavy-set blonde.

"Nice to meet you," Scott said, his voice sounding less than friendly.

Daron didn't take offense. The security personnel were concerned that they might not have a job in the coming weeks.

"Adesh is the head of security." Vikkas motioned to the dark-olive man leaving the center station. "He'll get you the list of the men's work schedule."

"You can take my station but there's no footage from the shooting." Adesh led him to the middle console. "I'm close to the family and I've been here for years. I've never seen anything like this happen. The system was down twenty minutes before and twenty after those guys left the premises."

Adesh logged in as Vikkas swept out of the room. "Let me know if you need anything else," he called over his shoulder.

"I'll get that list for you." Adesh walked away, leaving Daron at the center station.

When Daron went into the system, he found there had been an update and the footage from the day was in a backup file. A blessing because the video had not gone down until the actual reboot and was the first thing to come back online.

Daron watched the screen, taking in the series of events— Vikkas patting his pocket and walking away. Khalil tripping over the carpet gave the intruder the advantage. The gunman firing several shots. Vikkas hitting the assailant then jumping in front of Khalil. The intruder taking the center mass shot and the gun jamming. The intruders sprinting off before the police arrived. Daron reviewed footage of a patrol car entering the driveway and someone running out of another exit of the building, snagging their attention.

Who heard the shots and called the police? He was trying to process everything else he'd seen when Adesh returned.

"Oh! There is footage from the shooting," Adesh shocked, leaned closer to the screen.

"Rewind it." Daron shifted to allow Adesh closer access to gauge his reaction. "Show me from a few minutes before this."

Adesh hesitated, then said, "The young Mr. Germaine instructed if the footage was to be recovered to show you from this point forward." He tapped the screen that only showed Khalil laying in Vikkas' arms.

"I work for Khalil, not Vikkas, and if you know what's good for you … And for you to keep your job ..."

Adesh grumbled but complied. The footage, while in reverse, was a blur.

Kaleb Valentine. What the hell was he doing at The Castle? At no time had Kaleb mentioned he was there when they were attacked. Vikkas didn't mention it either.

"Fast forward."

Adesh shifted the speed.

"Stop."

Vikkas was holding Khalil in his arms, but a heated conversation took place between Kaleb and Vikkas before Kaleb stormed out of The Castle.

Interesting, it seems people are keeping secrets.

"I also need a list of personnel who weren't here on the day of the upgrade," Daron requested. He noticed Scott and Terrell kept an eye on him as Daron procured the printout from Adesh. Scott marched to a terminal as Terrell quickly slid out the door.

Daron returned his attention to the screen, then cursed while reviewing the coding that rebooted the system. Cedric, his resident hacker, was the person who took down the system. Daron avoided having a conversation with Vikkas about his findings for a multitude of reasons. Most people wouldn't be receptive to being lenient on Cedric, considering what resulted from his action.

He gathered the items he needed and headed to the parking lot to find a slim, short man with wide blue eyes, thin lips, and sunburnt skin— who had an intense glare—leaning on the Porsche. Marquise Sinclair.

"It seems your hearing isn't too good." Marquise stalked toward him with two goons nipping at his heels.

"You're the one with the problem." Daron stepped in his face, undeterred by being outnumbered. "The answer is still no."

"If that's your final answer," Marquise growled, shoulder bumping Daron as he continued to a Bentley Flying Spur. He stood in the open door. "Enjoy that beautiful woman of yours while you can."

CHAPTER 8

An hour later, Daron waited for Cedric to arrive as Brandi sent another one of his calls straight to voicemail. He left the voicemail Cameron suggested as the security tablet started beeping. He reached for the device, watching as Cedric slipped in through the side door and down to the basement.

"What's up, Mr. Dee?" Cedric's approach was slow, almost overly cautious. He paused at his normal workstation.

"You hacked into The Castle system, getting two men shot and one almost killed." Daron leaned on the big wood desk at the back area hating that he was here having this conversation.

Cedric's focus went to the ground. "I accepted the job before I met you."

"The man who was shot had only been back in town for three weeks at the time." Daron was curious about how far in advance this event was planned. He made a mental note to ask Nicco to follow up with Khalil about when he decided to end his world tour and return home, and who else was aware of his plans.

"Well, they knew because I was hired long before that." Cedric pulled a laptop out of his messenger bag. "Mr. Dee, I swear it was one of the last jobs I had to complete before I got out of that life." His fingers flew over the keys, then he flipped the screen toward Daron.

"How did you get past the firewall so quickly to reset the system?"

"One of the security guards gave me the IP address to the terminal and granted me remote access to the system." Cedric then explained it would have made it difficult and time-consuming to get in otherwise. "I was instructed to manually reboot the system since attempting to shut it down would trigger alarms."

Daron frowned as he asked, "Were you informed of the upgrade to the system that was done two days prior?" The answer to this question was key in narrowing down the suspect list.

Cedric shook his head, frowning as though he'd just been cursed out. "Are you going to turn me in?"

"Not if you tell me the name of the security personnel who was assisting you." Daron retrieved the cell from his jacket pocket.

He put a hand over Daron's cell. "I don't know," he confessed. "For my safety, I keep all communications digital, never in person."

Daron peered at the young man, taking in eyes, stance, and demeanor. He had a feeling Cedric didn't tell him everything. "I'm sorry to have to do this."

"Wait. Wait." He waved both hands frantically as Daron stood. "The only thing I know was he wasn't working *that* day. I had to make sure I could access the system fifteen minutes before I reset it."

Daron could work with that but he remained silent for a few moments to let Cedric sweat. "Look, we're going to keep this between us. However, if I find out you've taken another assignment ..."

Cedric was the one participant who didn't have to continue working jobs during the transition. He was his own boss, unlike Reese and Amarion who had fallen under Marquise's radar at an age too young to comprehend the consequences.

"I won't. Pedro's set me up with a contact out of DC who's looking for someone with my skills." Cedric collected the laptop, typing again before closing and tucking it under his arm. "He pays well and is willing to work with my schedule if I choose to take classes."

Daron's cell pinged. "You'd better have your ass in school. Don't make me regret this."

Cedric slid past him then turned back when he reached the door and insisted, "You won't."

He checked his messages, buying a few moments for Cedric to clear the grounds, and found an email with the IP address that had been used to take the system down. Daron sent Nicco a text to track down the terminal and all the personnel with access. He'd cross-checked the list with people who were scheduled off on the upgrade day to further reduce the pool of potential culprits. Somehow that exchange between Kaleb and Vikkas didn't sit well. Had Vikkas put out a hit on his own father? If he did, his argument with Kaleb couldn't have been about that. Khalil was conscious when it happened.

Daron called Steve to get an update and find out about Brandi.

"Your Aunt Bee's making her rounds but at least she isn't making waves," Steve replied.

"I'll take that." Daron slipped behind the wheel, starting the engine. "At least I don't need bail money today."

Several minutes later, Daron disconnected the line as his tires rolled to a stop on the driveway. The television blared the sounds of an action scene from the entertainment room when he entered the house. He was grateful Cameron wasn't in the kitchen as he slipped into the office. He smiled, thinking about how animated she became when she was watching those kinds of films. Daron opened the safe, put in the external drive, and noticed the envelope from Marquise.

Marquise doesn't understand hitting me directly is a thousand times safer than targeting my woman.

Daron would send his enemy to prison. Cameron would put him six feet under if Marquise fooled around and unleashed Kimura, the hit woman within Cameron.

And if he actually managed to hurt her, then Daron would make him wish he was dead. It didn't help the two of the young men in his program, who were employed by Marquise.

As he closed the safe, Cameron's question about Bishop's letter popped into his mind. He retrieved the thick white envelope and tore it open.

Daron sank into the leather chair as he absorbed the words. He couldn't believe the contents but at the same time, he couldn't deny the truth. Pulling out his cell, he snapped a picture of the last two pages, then folded the papers and stuffed them back into the locked space. It wouldn't be wise to have them in hand if Cameron were to make an appearance.

He stared at the colorful abstract painting that hid the safe, trying to process that people had been hunting for one of Cameron's aliases ever since she'd gotten shot and almost died several years ago. Prior to Bishop's death, he had partnered up with an individual who was determined to find the culprit. They'd found a possible connection to The Castle. He was all for Bishop's request to watch over Cameron but the secrecy could put an end to their relationship. But learning this reinforced that he'd made the right decision to participate and be a part of Khalil's alliance to change the direction of the Castle.

Daron reviewed the list of people the two men had taken down in an attempt to get closer to the real person pulling the strings behind the curtain.

"Daron," Cameron called out. "Are you going to make me come get you? If I wanted to watch a movie alone, I'd be at my house."

"Here I come." Daron glanced around the office. He did something that he hadn't done while in the house. He set the alarm on the painting covering the safe. If Cameron entered, he would know.

She couldn't know what was in that letter. Ever.

CHAPTER 9

Cameron wrapped up a private session with a female attorney, whose schedule wouldn't allow her to make the self-defense class at its regular time. Since Calvin and Daron were working at the house, Mia had kindly offered to be the person that actually executed the demonstration with a client. It allowed Cameron to give her client more precise corrections.

Mia had gone into the women's locker area to change while Cameron walked the client to the door. She observed the lawyer as she climbed into her Lexus and drove off. Cameron returned to the room to gather her things. She paused and her instincts kicked in. Multiple feet sliding across the linoleum tiles. Strange because it was multiple. Normally only one person would check in at the end of the class. It immediately put her on high alert. *Was Levi finally making a move?*

"Your man isn't here to protect you this time." The same three men from the garage incident stepped into the room, looking like the muscle-bound version of the music group, Bell Biv DeVoe, as the one she dubbed Ricky closed the door.

This must be about whatever Daron was into before Levi targeted him.

"You were given the wrong impression." Cameron calmly zipped up her jacket. "He was trying to save your behinds, not mine."

"We saw your little *self-defense* moves." The tallest of the three, who was now Ronnie in her mind, stepped forward. "You need more than that to take us down."

The other two laughed.

"Clearly you're not planners." Cameron placed her gym bag down on the mat, wondering what happened to Mia. "How are you going to get me out of the front door?"

The shortest of the bunch she called Mike laughed. "We want to be seen. Someone needs to inform Daron you're gone."

Ricky leaned on the metal door as if to block her exit.

"You want to fight me?" Cameron smiled sweetly as she eyed the folding chair near the door. "Let's do this."

She hit Mike, who was closest to her, with three quick jabs then kicked him in the chest sending him sailing backward. Ronnie fired several punches, catching her in the abdomen, then sent a fist flying toward her face. She ducked under Ronnie's hand, punched him in the chest, then dropped to her knees spinning toward the chair. She popped up, snatched and closed the metal chair then swung it, hitting Ronnie in the head. His body hit the floor with a reassuring thud. Cameron opened the chair, using it to trap Ricky's slender muscular frame against the door before he could deliver a punch.

"I don't think so." She released the chair, closed it flat and slammed it against Ricky's abs. Ronnie captured her by her waist as she took another swing. The chair slipped out her hands clanking as it made contact with the floor.

"Ain't so tough now," Ronnie growled.

She jammed her elbow into the side of his head in three quick successions. Cameron shifted to the side to get a direct hit to the center of his throat. She grabbed the knife strapped to her ankle, slicing into Ronnie's thigh then his arm as Mike approached. Ronnie immediately released her. She landed a solid kick to Mike's face then issued a sidekick to Ronnie's gut, sending them both to the floor.

"Do you want to bleed today, gentlemen?" She pointed the knife at Ricky who was inching toward her. "Because this is your last opportunity to leave in one piece."

"We may have underestimated you," Ronnie confessed as he and Mike struggled to their feet. "Now we won't go easy on you."

"Good, because that was just me playing around." Cameron reached her left hand into her pocket. "This is me being serious." She whipped out the gold rod, extended it to full staff, then triggered the blades as she twirled it. Cameron was hoping not to leave the place a bloody mess but she'd do what she needed to do.

She slammed the wand down on Mike's arm causing him to let loose several obscenities then kicked Ricky in the face. Ronnie tackled her, trying to knock the wand out her hand. Cameron brought the blade down on Ronnie's shoulder as his body pressed her to the floor. Ronnie grunted and he held his mouth tight as though to keep from screaming.

Mia slipped across the threshold, snatching up the chair from the floor and slamming it down on Ronnie's back. "Couldn't let you have all the fun."

Ronnie rolled off Cameron. Ricky lunged at Mia, getting clipped in the chin as she went to take another swing.

The door banged against the wall, drawing their attention. "I'm sorry Miss Cameron, I thought you were finished in here." Larry, the facility manager, entered the room.

Ronnie stood, nodding toward the door. "We'll finish this conversation another time. Sweet cheeks."

Cameron retracted her wand, glancing at the few splatters of blood on the floor. "Larry, I'm finished with them."

Mia smiled, sweetly leaning the chair against the wall. Larry's eyes went to the bloodstain on Ronnie's arm, then his leg. The three men crossed the threshold with Cameron steps behind them as they enter the hallway, making sure they didn't try anything stupid.

They better be glad I'm retired, otherwise I'd track them down and make them wish they'd never come at me.

As they neared the exit, a little boy no more than twelve ran up to them. Ronnie rubbed his head then slipped him money before sliding out the door. Cameron checked the announcement board wondering if some of the activities were how they found the people to traffick.

"Is this fall out from Daron working with Calvin?" Mia asked, as Cameron returned to grab her bag.

"I don't think so." Cameron waved to Larry as they left the building. "Daron's latest tracker helped locate a missing girl so fast, police and the media were all over it. It's probably more about that." *Or whatever else has caused Daron's Warden persona to return.*

Calvin drove up less than a second after Mia opened the passenger door. "It looks like I don't need that ride after all. Be safe."

"You too." Cameron waved at Calvin as he drove off with a familiar black sedan trailing him.

Since Linc was in a separate car, there was no immediate threat. The security detail was a precaution. If Linc had been in the same vehicle, then it would've increased the possibility of Mia's concerns being correct. At first, Cameron had thought the incident at the garage had been about the Katara-Tracy situation. Daron was usually honest about the Calvin project. If he couldn't tell her specifics, he'd mention just that. Daron had recognized at least one of the guys who followed them. She hoped he wasn't caught in his old life.

Ten minutes later, she parked a couple of blocks away and walked up Longwood to Daron's house. Daron insisted on escorting her to the car if she left late, which grated on her nerves at first. She wasn't accustomed to anyone beside her small cluster of friends and crew being concerned for her well-being. But for safety reasons, she parked somewhere different every time she visited. Only when she knew she wasn't staying the night did she park at the back of the house so that he'd have only a short distance to walk. She pulled her baseball cap low over her forehead and sported a plain jogging suit. Cameron hustled up the hill to the front door, not even trying to avoid the sensor this time.

Daron opened the door wearing a pair of dark-gray slacks and a black shirt. He leaned down, planting a kiss on her lips before sliding the bag from her shoulder and letting her through the door.

"It smells good up in here." Cameron slipped her shoes off. "How did things go with Calvin?"

"Productive." Daron wrapped his arm around her waist, nuzzling her neck. "Since we're not hanging with your friends tonight, I thought maybe we could eat in."

Tonight was her evening to pick the activity. Most times she chose to hang with the family of her crew, Greg and Rob. Now that they didn't work together, she rarely saw them. She tried to catch up with them for basketball, bowling, or a game night. They had taken her exit from the business better than she expected.

"Sounds great. Let me shower and change." She slid out of his arms then smiled, giving him an appreciative once over. "Maybe you should slip into something sexy for me."

"Exactly what would that be?" he teased.

"Get creative." Cameron winked as she headed to the shower.

"How about I join you?" Daron called after her.

"Did you make that cantaloupe drink? 'Cause if you didn't, you have work to do." Cameron said, knowing if he joined her in the shower they would have a late dinner. She was famished.

She stripped, turned on the warm water and stepped under the stream. Normally she wouldn't mind but with that little episode at the center earlier, they needed to talk. She was out of the shower within minutes and was dressed when the door opened.

"Damn, Cam. That was the quickest shower ever." Daron leaned in the doorway, wearing only his silk boxers.

"Aren't you supposed to be making my drink?" She shoved him gently out of the doorway. "Did you make dessert?"

He glanced back at her. "You are my dessert."

"Mmm," she mused. "Well, you'll have to get that *after* dinner." Cameron guided a playfully reluctant Daron into the dining room, before taking a seat at the square walnut table. "How was the earlier part of your day?"

"Busy, but I crossed a lot off my list." Daron talked about the changes to his programs, upgrading some tech gear and a few elements of working on Calvin's project.

Once Daron finished putting more Chicken Kare Kare on his plate and poured the last of the cantaloupe juice into her glass, she asked, "Is everything else all right?"

He stopped mid-bite. "What do you mean?"

She shrugged, weighing her next words carefully. "Three men visited me this evening planning to kidnap me to send you a message. I was wondering if they sent you another one earlier."

"What?" Daron's fork clicked against a blue over-sized bowl as he reached for the cell that had been vibrating on the table on and off all night. "Why didn't you say something when you first came home?"

She placed her hand over his as he unlocked the cell, undoubtedly to call Steve. "I planned to, then I got here and it was smelling so good. My stomach said it could wait. I figured we could discuss it over dinner."

"Do not wait to tell me something like that, Babe." Daron leaned toward, the concern in his eyes made her heart soften a bit. "I want to know as soon as you get somewhere safe. Was it Levi?"

"No, the same men that approached us when we left the Cheesecake Factory," Cameron said, referring to the garage incidents that happen weeks ago then took a breath. She was still getting adjusted to being with him and having to answer to anyone in this way. "Telling you sooner isn't an unreasonable request."

He leaned in, resting his forehead against hers. "That wasn't a request. That was an order." He smiled as she frowned.

Daron was messing with her, knowing she hated when people barked orders, even though he *was* serious. "Are *you* going to call *me* when stuff like that happens to you?"

The oven dinged.

"Let me grab dessert." He moved quickly into the kitchen.

"I can still hear you from there, so answer the question."

Daron pulled the pan from the oven and set it on the stovetop. "Do you want some wine since we're out of juice?" He motioned toward the empty pitcher on the table, then pulled out a bottle of Riesling and glasses.

"I take you avoiding answering me as a no." She finished off the juice and he replaced it with wine. "But we will discuss it further when you least expect it and I'm not in the mood to let you sidestep."

Daron leaned over and kissed her cheek. "I'd tell you." As he sat down, he whispered "Eventually."

"I heard that."

"I'm going to have Steve put a protection detail on you," Daron stated, sliding a fork full of chicken into his mouth.

"Do you have one?" she shot back.

He took his time before answering. "We're talking about you."

"But you're the one they're really trying to send that message. I'm just the conduit. Eventually, they'll come directly for you."

"Accept the detail, Cam," Daron demanded along with a stern authoritative glare.

"No," she countered. "Not unless you do the same."

"Babe, I don't want to argue with you." Daron's lips were curled upward in a forced smile but his hand had a death grip on the fork. "It's happening."

"Not in this lifetime." She stuffed a bite into her mouth. "Man, you'd better be glad you can cook because I will tell you *Mr. I Run Things,* I'm not one of your employees. You can't boss me around or issue demands and expect me to comply. I'd leave but I'm trying to get a second plate."

Daron chuckled and his hand relaxed a little. "Think about it." He lifted her hand from the table and placed it in his. "If anything happens to you because of me. I'd never forgive myself."

"Don't try to be sly about it and your people end up dead, attempting to discreetly follow me."

"I can't make that promise." Daron gave her a half-smile, then he seemed to become lost in thought for a moment, which meant he was creating a strategy to do exactly what she asked him not to do. That determination in Daron's eyes let Cameron know she'd have a difficult time getting him to let it go. The last thing she wanted was that damn ghost drone following her around.

"Warden, are you back in business? Is that why I suddenly need a detail?"

Daron's head snapped toward her. "Calvin's project—"

"Has its dangers, but it's not currently what's causing the problem. Otherwise, Calvin's detail would be sharing a car. Despite Mia being on your roster, you'd have someone watching over her. So why are men coming after me to get to you?"

Daron's gaze landed on the wall. He placed the fork on the edge of the bowl, abandoning all efforts to finish dinner. "Calvin isn't the one who they're trying to get to stop working on the project." Daron's jaw tightened as he spoke. Although he was looking her in the eyes, he wasn't really focused on her.

Cameron sighed. *Another half-truth.*

Daron stood, his steely gaze landed on her briefly as he gathered the bowl and the pitcher.

He gave her his back to ponder. Not a good sign.

The conversation was definitely over, for now.

CHAPTER 10

The shrill of Daron's cell ringing for the fourth time cut through the silence. Cameron refused to open her eyes as he shifted to answer. They'd only been sleeping for a few hours after an intense make-up session.

"Do you realize what time it is?" Daron carefully slid his arm from under her head and sat up in the bed. His groggy voice lowered to barely a whisper. "There's no business that needs to be handled at this time of morning." He left the bed and the room.

The naked sculpture of his body in the hallway provided a visual but she couldn't hear much of his side. Body language alone said it wasn't good. He came back in, got dressed in the dark, then kissed her on the forehead. "Babe, I have to run out for a couple of hours."

"Be safe," she said as he swept his prototype watch off the nightstand.

The lights dimmed as he crept out. Cameron rolled over, glancing at the clock and trying to figure out where he could possibly be going at three-thirty in the morning. She contemplated following but figured she'd at least give him a chance to come home and explain before making that kind of move. Her eyes closed but she couldn't sleep. The silent battle began in her head.

Why didn't he grab his usual watch? Do not follow him.

She had promised herself that she'd judge each man on his actions but it was harder than she thought. The past created new insecurities and cautions. These last few weeks had triggered some of them. Cameron wanted to trust him, but people did things they claimed they'd never do all the time. Situations spiraled out of control.

Maybe the lies aren't intentional. Maybe Daron is lying to himself about the situation and passing that lie on to me.

One thing she learned from her ex, was she couldn't allow anyone to pull her down to their level. When it came to the non-negotiable things in life, they had to be willing to step up or she'd be forced to leave them behind. If Daron wasn't planning to remain retired, she needed to part ways before he dragged her back into the life she had escaped.

You want him to trust you. You have to give him a chance to tell you in his own time. Unless the attacks continue.

A buzzing noise filled the air. Cameron shot up in the bed. The tablet on the nightstand flashed as the buzzing went quiet and the alarm sounded. She swiped to open it and saw a dark figure with a duffel bag approaching the house. The alarm system changed the setting of the lights to record. The bedroom light went from completely off to a dim glow which she knew continued throughout the rest of the house. She slipped out of the bed, pulled on a pair of jogging pants, shirt, and grabbed her gun. She peeked at the screen. Daron's first alarm had been disengaged, causing his secondary system to kick in. Cameron pressed the button to prevent Daron's door shield from activating. She wanted to see exactly what this fool was trying to do.

The masked man entered the back door, wandering around the living room before he dropped the bag on the floor then rushed into Daron's office. He spent a few minutes there ransacking the drawers before exploring the basement. Twenty minutes later he made his way back upstairs, grabbing the duffel bag and heading into the kitchen.

"Unbelievable," Cameron whispered as he helped himself to the remaining piece of her cheesecake from the refrigerator.

The man lifted the delicious bite to his mouth again, taking another one before sitting it right next to the duffel bag. After wiping his gloved hand on a paper towel, he opened the cabinet and a wicked smile crossed his face. He retrieved a clear sleeve from the black bag he had dropped on the island top with what she assumed was cocaine. Cameron dialed the oldest of her three brothers, lowering the sound on the phone as she tipped out of the bedroom. She placed the phone on a table in the hallway when her brother answered and prayed he could hear.

"You must not know whose house you're in." She leaned on the wall with the Ruger hidden behind her back. "Did you think you were going to plant drugs here and get away with it?"

"I'm DEA." He snatched off his mask and knocked the duffel bag to the floor as he lifted one of the white packages. "I just found this."

"Bull. I have a recording that says otherwise," she countered. "But why don't you call my brother, Justin." Cameron smiled sweetly as fear lit in his eyes. "He's DEA, too."

He shifted around to the front of the island, "It's interesting that you're sleeping with a drug dealer considering what your brother does." He lifted the gun. "It's unfortunate that you are."

Cameron had to handle things carefully since Daron's system was recording everything. However, she wasn't trying to get shot. But if the man left the house and managed to escape, there wouldn't be a clear shot of his face based on when he snatched off his mask. "So, Mr. DEA agent. How would Justin feel about you planting drugs at my boyfriend's house and murdering his baby sister?"

"As if he'd ever know."

"Do you know what Daron's specialty is, sweetie?" She stepped forward keeping the gun hidden behind her thigh. Whatever business that *had* Daron out of bed this early had to be cut short and he was on his way back. Since the intruder barely waited thirty minutes after Daron left to make his move, Daron would soon be making an appearance.

"No one will get to you in time." He moved around the island. "I suggest you stop advancing."

Her steps halted. "Where's your team?" Cameron put the free hand on her hip, being careful not to shift her eyes to the flicker of a shadow that crossed the threshold.

His forehead had deep crease lines and beads of sweat as he seized the bag's strap. "Move toward the back door slowly."

"Okay." Cameron kept her back to the wall and her eyes focused on the agent.

Let the fun begin.

Daron placed his Beretta to the DEA agent's head. "You'll never get the shot off in time."

The agent dropped his weapon but swung the bag up at Daron, knocking the Beretta out of Daron's hand. Cameron whipped the Ruger out but didn't have a shot as the two of them wrestled to reach the gun. Their hands knocked into the agent's weapon, sending it twirling across the floor.

The agent punched Daron in the ribs.

Daron slammed a fist into the ivory cheek four times until it became red. He rammed a knee into the man's abs, sending him gliding across the dining room floor. The agent quickly got to his feet and lunged for Daron.

Daron slammed his hand down on the face of the watch then two probes shot out, hitting the man in the chest. The man's body went still as the voltage hit him, causing him to fall onto Daron.

I definitely need to add a taser watch to my collection. Cameron was already thinking of the modification for the device. She didn't like the fact that the wires were still connected to the watch.

Daron pushed the man off, flipped him face down on the ground, placed a knee in his back while folding both arms together to keep him secured. He glanced up at her. "Are you okay?"

Cameron nodded as she pressed the Ruger against the agent's forehead. "What were you saying about no one getting to me in time?"

CHAPTER 11

A DEA agent attempting to plant drugs on Daron and Cameron and two separate attacks so soon after Marquise's threat was not a coincidence. The fact that the agent planted them in his personal residence and not the other house indicated this move was tied to Calvin's project. Marquise clearly had decent federal connections.

He hated that last night was his first official introduction to Cameron's brother, Justin. She had the presence of mind to skillfully setup the rogue agent's takedown and big brother came in like the cavalry. The one good thing with Justin handling the agent's arrest was Daron knew the incident couldn't be stuffed in a back closet as if it never happened.

Daron refocused on Steve. "How's Aunt Bee doing? Cam and I are having an early dinner with her tonight."

"Your aunt's been approaching Bishop's former associates," Steve stated, retrieving a tablet from his messenger bag. "How much do you know about her?"

Daron gripped the tablet as the pictures came through. "Is she trying to get herself killed?"

"I came in town to handle it because there's more to your aunt's queries than just Troy. Flip to the last picture." He waited until Daron swiped through. "You don't pull a gun on a woman unless you feel she's a real threat."

"Damn." Daron suspected Brandi thought Roger was responsible, but this suggests a bigger issue.

"She knows something, even though we know he couldn't have had anything to do with Troy's," he used air quotes, "accident."

"Find out what he did that makes her suspect him." Daron leaned back in the chair, Brandi might not be his favorite person, but he didn't want her dead. "Shit, retirement has been busier than expected and much more dangerous than being The Warden."

"I'm on it," Steve said, laughing.

Daron alarm beeped, alerting him to Cameron's arrival. He made his way to open the door with Steve on his tail. Daron attempted to keep his expression neutral as a surge of lust and desire hit him like a lightning bolt. Cameron approached, wearing a form-fitting navy dress and stilettos. He hadn't expected her to be in workout gear to meet his aunt but damn if he didn't want to kick Steve out and cancel all plans that didn't involve the two of them alone.

"Hey, beautiful."

She slid past him before he could get a good hold on her. "Lex mentioned you were up this way." She hugged Steve, a little too long for Daron's taste.

Lex was actually Daron's friend. He and Cameron bonded over the summer and she maintained the platonic relationship, not realizing Lex would have given up his playboy status for her. Daron didn't need the turbulence in their relationship to give her a new appreciation of Lex when Daron was being pulled in several different directions.

"Your man doesn't understand that his transition requires him to remain in the shadows." Steve ignored Daron's evil glare, giving Cameron another tight squeeze before releasing her.

"Tell me about it," she mumbled, tossing a smile Daron's way.

"I'm in the room." Daron was not fond of Steve's close proximity to Cameron but he knew by the glint in Steve's eye he was intentionally taunting with him.

"Try to keep this one out of trouble," Steve said as he moved toward the door.

"You're asking a lot." Cameron pursed her chocolate lips and cut those dark-brown contact covered eyes at Daron as he pushed Steve out the door.

"I'll see you later," Daron said, waving. "Thanks for coming up."

Steve could be heard laughing as he walked away.

Daron watched as Steve made his way over to his truck, appreciating the fact that Steve drove almost two hours to personally handle this situation.

Daron didn't care for the distance between him and Cameron that was developing so quickly. Men were already waiting in the wings hoping for an opportunity to be with her. Two of which were in their inner circle.

Cameron was a wild card and Daron didn't know how far her "dude-like qualities" as Bishop described them, went. The one thing he knew was once he won her heart and trust, he didn't have to worry about anything else. Until then, he wasn't taking any chances. Daron wanted Cameron in his life. In regard to their relationship, the timing couldn't have been worse to become a King of The Castle, have Marquise coming for him, along with the complications of dealing with Levi.

"Did Steve look into your list of candidates for your project?" Cameron asked as Daron wrapped his arm around her waist.

"We should cancel with my aunt and eat in." Daron lowered his lips to hers.

She pulled back, patting him on the chest. "Mmm, seeing that we have just enough time to drive to meet her, canceling is out of the question."

"She's closer to the restaurant." He retrieved his cell.

"We're not canceling." Cameron reached for the door handle. "I want to meet this aunt of yours."

Daron collected his suit jacket from the couch and keys off the kitchen counter. "Fine, but don't forget about the charity event." He'd invited Cameron to join him but she opted for dropping him off and picking him up later.

Brandi had been ignoring his calls and voicemails ever since he'd broken up her fight with Roger's lady friend.

Cameron suggested that Daron leave Brandi a message about meeting his girlfriend. Of course, his aunt responded to that and this was the only day she was available.

After Daron secured the house, Cameron followed him to the Porsche. "You can answer my question about the candidates."

He slipped behind the wheel and started his journey to Wishbone Restaurant. "He's working on it. We have the list down to three people who all will be attending the event tonight. Steve has a team looking into each one."

"Can I ask you why you're so passionate about helping these young men?" Cameron turned down the light jazz that was playing on the radio. "It's not like you were *that* kid."

Daron merged onto the I-57. "And my parents worked hard to keep me from being *that* kid. When my brother turned to that life after my father's death, I realized that the street will offer them whatever they feel like they're lacking to lure them in."

"Every boy doesn't want to be saved from the streets." Cameron shifted, adjusting the seatbelt more comfortably over her breasts.

Daron eased on the brakes as the traffic grew thicker the closer they came to downtown. He could feel the heat of her glare on his face.

"Bishop lived and breathed for that."

Daron agreed and glanced at her before merging into the express lanes. "There are a lot of JD's out there caught up in the life, who bury their dreams because they feel like the streets are their only option."

"Mmm." She touched the control, increasing the volume of the music.

Daron glanced over to see Cameron staring out of the window. "Speak your truth, Cam."

She didn't bother to look his way. "What if a Bishop rolls through your program?"

A call rang through the Bluetooth, Daron tapped the word decline on the screen.

Seconds later, her phone chimed. Cameron reached into the clutch to silence the tone. "Some people may enter to get close to you to get what you have."

She had a point. "So far Pedro's psychological evaluations have been efficient at weeding out individuals without the qualities to succeed in a program like mine." Daron finally understood her concern. She was the person Bishop sent in on the hardest assignments. "Sweetheart, if we make it public, there will be no direct access to me anymore."

"And you think making it public will reduce the ripples of effect on your life?"

"Yes." Daron exited the expressway. He checked the rearview, making sure no one was tailing him. "It's why I need to select the correct person to be the face of the program. They'll be taking the praise and the heat. If they're truly passionate and love what they do, then they'll be able to navigate the challenges that are expected at the beginning."

"I want you to consider expanding your vision in order to widen your net," Cameron said as he quickly parked in an empty spot on a street near the restaurant.

He smiled at her words, rounded the car and opened her door. "What's your idea?"

"Give *all* kids somewhere safe to go after school. That way, students doing well continue to do so and those in your *special* program can be discreet."

"I love that idea." Cameron constantly helped him up his game. He appreciated that the majority of the time she simply made a suggestion or asked him to take another look at his plans without nitpicking.

"Daron, can you save the make-out session until *after* you introduce us and we eat?"

Something heavy hit his back.

Cameron chuckled and put a few inches between them.

"Aunt Bee. This is Cameron." Daron turned to find Brandi in a bright lime suit with a silver sequined tank peeking through. She looked more like a 70's disco queen than a woman hitting a senior citizen stride. His eyes went to his aunt's oversized Chanel purse.

"You can call me Brandi." She looped an arm under Cameron's, guiding her to the door. Her reddish-brown skin contrasted with Cameron's light tone. "No wonder his ass didn't call me when he got back into town."

Daron held the door then followed the ladies in, glad there were seats available. The scent inside the restaurant immediately reminded him of soul food Sundays with his family before his father died. His friends used to tease him about his Filipino mother cooking soul food. They didn't realize she was raised down south where most of the Filipino population settled on the East and West Coast. While her mother was Filipino and her dad was Caucasian, Theresa spent a lot of time with her Godmother who owned a restaurant that specialized in southern cuisine. The one thing Theresa did not do was play when it came to food, his father and her children.

"Troy, Shane, and Daron, when they were young were always getting into something." Brandi sat her bag in the empty chair next to her. "The stories I could tell."

"She's more interested in knowing about you." Daron's cell vibrated in the pocket of his slacks. He wondered if Nicco's team had completed the interviews of the seven Castle staff who were suspected of helping Cedric. Not thinking, he checked the message to see if a notification of the results had come through. Cameron placed a palm over the screen then slid a menu in front of him.

"Nonsense." Brandi glanced over the menu.

"Ha, nice try." Cameron gave him a wicked glare, tightening her hand on his. "I love to hear all about his adventures."

Daron cut his eyes over at Cameron, who winked at him. He caught the waitress' attention with his free hand and waved her over.

"Did he tell you the story about how he almost got his brother and Shane in trouble for drinking his father's specialty beer?"

Cameron bumped his shoulder with hers and loosened her hold on him. "You don't say."

The petite waitress came to the table. "You're ready to order?"

"Yes," Daron responded, ordering the crab cakes, blackened chicken breast, mashed sweet potatoes and the red beans and rice, then making sure Cameron tried the southern fried catfish, collard greens and macaroni & cheese.

"Could I have the Cajun shrimp and grits but without the sautéed mushrooms? Could I add sautéed bacon, and get a couple of lemon wedges on the side." Brandi dismissed the waitress with a wave of her multi-ringed fingers.

Cameron's smile disappeared and Daron sighed. He had selected Wishbone because his aunt was notorious for de-constructing an entree and building it into something different. He was praying they cooked it right or she'd get belligerent and send it back.

"So how have you been?" Daron slid his cell from the table back into his pocket. "When does Shane get back into town?"

Brandi flicked her jet-black hair over her shoulder. "I didn't forget what I was talking about."

"How about you tell us how you're doing first?" Daron wanted to extend the conversation as long as he could. The beer story wasn't the most embarrassing one she could tell but she did have a few that he'd prefer never reach Cameron's ears.

"So, Darius had this expensive beer and when he picked it up to drink—" Brandi waved him off as she pulled out a cell, "—It was gone. He just knew it was Troy or Shane."

"Well, I know who the culprit was. How old was he?" Cameron placed an arm on the back of his chair and accepted the phone Brandi extended her way. She stared at the picture of Troy, Shane, and Daron when they were younger.

"Three or four." Brandi mouthed a thank you as the waitress sat a glass of water in front of her. "Daron was underneath the bed. Every time his dad set the beer down, he'd sip out of it."

"Adorable." Cameron returned the cell. "How did he find out it was Daron?"

Brandi dropped the cell back into her bag. "He'd caught Troy and Shane at the foot of the bed. If Daron hadn't belched, Darius would've never known he was hiding."

Cameron chuckled. "I didn't know you were such a *smooth* criminal."

Daron didn't respond.

Brandi cackled with glee. "The foolishness the three of them would get into."

They did get into a lot of trouble together. Troy's motto was he had to be first and Daron had to make sure he was second. Daron laughed. "Those were good times."

Brandi also told the story of the time when he was injured skateboarding down one of the hills to Longwood, getting caught playing strip Uno and throwing a party while his parents were out on a date. She had Cameron in stitches.

"Your dad was always looking after me and Shane." She became teary-eyed, at the mention of Darius, then pushed back the chair and snatched up her purse. "I'll be back. I need to use the restroom."

"I'll go with you." Cameron was on her feet, trailing Brandi.

Daron glanced at the window, noticing one of Marquise's men approaching the restaurant while another was checking out the parked car. Quickly he rose to his feet but Roc, Brandi's, guardian, intercepted him, then Linc made a move on the other man.

His cell chimed with a message that the situation was handled. Daron lowered himself back onto the wooden seat. He sent a message to Roc to confirm that he didn't need to have someone else watch over Brandi. Daron assumed Linc was relieving Roc for them both to be there. His focus stayed divided between the direction the women went and out of the window.

By the time the police arrived, which he assumed Roc called, he realized quite a bit of time had passed. The food had been placed on the table and the women still hadn't returned. He texted Cameron, EVERYTHING OKAY. She replied. ON OUR WAY BACK.

Minutes later, they returned to the table. Daron noticed that Cameron kept the conversation general, talking about music and fashion. Aunt Bee wasn't her flamboyant self for a change. He couldn't wait to have a conversation with Cameron about what happened away from the table. Brandi was always over the top. She didn't bother to send her meal back to the kitchen. Daron settled the bill as they headed out of the restaurant.

"When Shane gets back, we should all get together," Daron suggested once they reached Brandi's BMW.

"Yeah," she answered half-heartedly, looking emotional.

He pulled Brandi in for a hug before she slid behind the wheel, then walked back to the Porsche to open Cameron's door. Once she was seated, he made his way to the driver's side. Daron waited until Brandi drove off before leaving, noticing that Linc was now following her.

"Damn," Cameron glanced at him, pulling out a mirror to reapply her chocolate lipstick. "I knew your brother was dead to the organization. I didn't realize he'd faked his death to make it happen."

Daron simply looked at her for a moment. He hadn't realized she'd known any part of that. He was relieved he could actually talk about it without revealing what he wasn't ready to tell her. "Yes, she's feeling guilty about his death and I can't convince her that it was an accident. And I can't tell her the truth either, I'll endanger Troy and his family's life."

Cameron looked in the direction Brandi had taken off.

"You need to figure out why she feels guilty over your father's death, then maybe you can find a way to help her accept that Troy's was truly an accident."

CHAPTER 12

Daron was hesitant to let Cameron drop him off at the reception. But he also didn't want her in the lobby bar either. Marquise was supposed to be attending this event. The last thing he needed was for his nemesis to happen to lay eyes on her. He pulled off Michigan Avenue in front of the luxury hotel.

"What are you planning to do while I'm here?" he asked, retrieving the suit jacket from the back seat.

"Going with you," Cameron smirked, daring him to protest. "I didn't wear this outfit for your aunt."

"Babe, you have made my night." Daron would've been worried about her the second she left his side.

He slid out and rounded the car to open the door but the doorman had already done the honors. Daron joined Cameron near the revolving door and they made their way up the large elegant staircase to the event in the grand ballroom. He'd purchased two tickets expecting Pedro to attend, but a friend who could help him with the evaluation of the women staying at Reno's shelter had an opening in his schedule. The results would determine which women would receive the tracking earrings and which ones would need an alternative device like a watch or bracelet.

Cameron springing this on him meant she was clearly up to something but he didn't care. Daron pulled Cameron close. When he spotted one of the program candidates, he positioned himself to have an opportunity to conduct an unofficial interview.

"I only have to be tied down with these stupid kids two more years before my father lets me into his company." A heavyset brown-haired man stroked his date's arm and continued to gripe about being there.

Daron maneuvered Cameron away since he was immediately crossing the man off the list and had no desire to speak to him. "Calvin and Mia should be here tonight."

"Mia mentioned Calvin liked to speak at youth programs." Cameron ordered a martini from the bar. "He's truly destroying my belief in tech guys being nerdy."

"What about me?"

"You're a techie or a nerd?"

"You got jokes." He networked his way toward the second candidate. Ralph Pullman looked distinguished in a black suit and with a few gray hairs in his fade that hinted he was older than his youthful skin suggested.

Daron introduced himself and Cameron. "Ralph, I'd love to hear more about what you do."

Cameron listened intently, interjecting by occasionally asking questions. Only one name remained on the list, Daron scanned the room. The woman either hadn't arrived yet or she was taking care of things in the background. Nothing was official until after the in-depth background checks came back and he decided on whether to present the proposal to them.

A dark-brown beauty wearing designer shades that covered the top part of her face smiled brightly as she crossed the threshold. Elegant in a Dior red dress that hugged her slender hourglass figure, she pulled off her spectacles, greeting the crowd near the door along with an alderman as though she was some type of celebrity.

Levi entered seconds later, stopping to talk to a senator.

The woman sidestepped the alderman, who entered with her, while both attempted to give the appearance of not knowing each other.

Daron had the feeling those two were an item or at least had been. The woman made a beeline for him and Cameron almost as if she had already been informed of their location. "Hello, I'm Alisha Roderick."

"Daron Kincaid." He slid his arm around Cameron's waist as he shook Alisha's hand. He focused as Levi faded into the crowd. "This is Cameron."

"Your face was familiar. I thought I'd introduce myself. I run a program for at-risk youth out of the Gresham neighborhood." She handed Daron a brochure. "What is it that you do?"

Daron could feel Cameron's eyes on him as she tensed. "I'm attending to support these organizations that give back to the community."

Cameron's cell chirped, but she ignored it, choosing to keep her attention on Alisha.

"Maybe you can come and check mine out one of these days." Alisha's smile brightened but her eyes were laser-focused on him in an almost predatory way.

"Tell me a little more about the program."

Daron listened as she explained what her organization did, but his eyes scanned the people milling about, hoping to keep tabs on Levi. She touched his arm several times during the explanation. Something he was sure Cameron didn't miss.

A bald Asian man tapped her on the shoulder and flickered a glance at him.

"Duty calls. Great meeting both of you." She lightly touched Daron's shoulder in a suggestive manner. "If you want to know more please stop by." Alisha followed the guy through the crowd.

Cameron sipped the martini she held. "Whatever you're here trying to accomplish, she's not the one. Especially if you're thinking about your program."

Daron stared at her for a moment thrown by the comment. "Why?"

"You're not the only one with ulterior motives for that little meet and greet." Cameron gestured to the pamphlet in his hand with a sticky note that contained Alisha's cell number.

"Maybe she ran out of business cards." Daron wanted to give her the benefit of the doubt since he hadn't seen Alisha write anything once she came through the door.

"Yeah right." Cameron's cell chirped again. "It's my mom. Let me step into the foyer and see what she wants."

Cameron was only gone for fifteen seconds before Alisha reappeared. "Has your friend stepped away?"

"Momentarily." Something about Ms. Roderick didn't feel right but he couldn't put his finger on it.

Meanwhile, Levi's movements through the ballroom demanded his attention.

"We're hosting a fundraiser to offset the cuts we received from the State. I'd love if *you* could come through and support." Alisha shifted, blocking his view of Levi when he had finally parted ways with the group.

"I'll think about it." Daron tapped the pamphlet against his hand, cutting his eyes at Levi, who seemed to have a pointed interest in them.

"You're very handsome," she said, placing her hands on his bicep. "And I think we'd make a great team on a more personal level."

"I'm with Cameron."

"But is she with you?" She glanced back at Cameron on the phone in the hallway just outside the door. Daron didn't know what his expression looked like but Alisha quickly blurted, "I'm sorry. I was hoping that it wasn't serious." She tucked her purse under her arm. "I'm hoping this won't affect you coming to check out what I do."

"No," Daron stated, not sure if he wanted a program director conducting herself in such a brazen manner. The boys were the focus, not what was between her thighs.

"Good, I thought I might have scared you off when I let you know I was interested in you. It wasn't my intent to make you … uncomfortable." Alisha stepped back. "Over the years, I've learned every woman on a man's arm is not a permanent fixture in his life."

"You don't have to explain." He wondered if he was judging her too harshly, thinking about all the males he'd seen flirting with wives and girlfriends over the years.

"I do and I realize some people feel it's disrespectful to go behind a woman's back to reveal an interest." Her smile dripped pure honey. "When a man doesn't specifically introduce the woman he's with as his *girlfriend*, there's a greater chance they're simply casually dating."

"As I said, an explanation is not necessary." He gave her a fake smile of his own. "I'll happily claim Cameron as my woman whether you ask in front of her or after she walks away but I can understand why you took that approach." Daron shot Cameron a "you can come back anytime" look but her back was turned to the ballroom. He saw Levi making his way across the floor like a man on the hunt.

Cameron was the target.

"She's a very lucky woman." Alisha rested a hand on his arm.

He glanced down at her hand for two seconds then back to Alisha's face. She quickly removed it. He doubted that Alisha missed that he avoided saying that Cameron was his woman. Either way, he'd had enough. Levi had been stopped by a community organizer seconds before he reached the door.

Daron had to admit that Cameron's instincts were spot on as he worked his way through the attendees. Cameron didn't strike him as the jealous type but he wasn't willing to find out the hard way. He knew exactly who he wanted to rule by his side and wake up to every morning. As if she felt him, Cameron's brown orbs locked onto his and she smiled, then slid her phone into her purse and headed his way.

"So, are there any other *candidates* we're checking out tonight?" Cameron slipped an arm around his waist. "Or checking you out?"

Levi excused himself from the group a few feet away. "Mrs. Kincaid, lovely seeing you again."

Daron held Cameron closer, ignoring the fact he'd only spoken to Cameron. "We can't say the same."

"*Dareen,*" Levi intentionally pronounced Daron's name wrong. "I only wanted to invite your Missus to check out my new restaurant opening in Lincoln Park." He extended a postcard with a gift card attached to Cameron.

Before Daron could snatch it up, Cameron said, "Keep it. I prefer *his* cooking along with everything else."

Daron normally would have been annoyed that Cameron didn't allow him to handle the situation. However, seeing the flare of frustration in Levi's eyes before Daron guided her away made all the difference in the world.

"Don't let him play games with you. Showing up at the center. Inviting me to his restaurant." Cameron stopped moving, wrapping both arms around his waist. "He's trying to throw you off your game before he attacks."

"Babe. I'm already at a disadvantage since I don't know why I've become his target." Daron planted a kiss on her lips and didn't miss that Alisha had made her way closer.

"Stop trying to figure that out and concentrate on taking him down." Cameron pushed back, staring deeply in his eyes.

He placed a kiss on her forehead as Calvin and Mia emerged from the crowd along with another couple. "Daron and Cameron, I want to officially introduce you to Pastor Tony Baltimore and his wife Kari."

"Pleasure to meet you." Daron gave the green-eyed man a firm handshake while Cameron greeted his lovely wife.

"Calvin has been telling us about your programs." Daron was a little surprised neither Calvin or Pedro mentioned Tony was a minister or that some of his initiatives had come out of a church.

"You're interested in knowing what qualities make the best candidate. The first piece of advice, make sure the person is understanding and compassionate and not just talented and skilled." Tony went on and told his story of being forced to work for a drug dealer and how prison changed his life and stopped him from running from his purpose. "Coming out, I had to hold my ground to maintain my new course, so I understand what the people participating are up against."

Kari shifted to allow a few of the guests to pass, then added, "It's important to show them an alternative to their current lifestyle so they can see the finish line and not lose sight of their dreams."

Cameron nodded, and for the first time genuinely seemed to be enjoying herself.

"Their ministry has created a safe haven in the community for victims of child sex-trafficking, sexual abuse, and other traumatic circumstances." Calvin smiled, tucking Mia closely into his side, but his gaze was on Cameron whose eyes were focused on the Pastor and his wife.

"You're also mentoring and providing scholarship programs, correct?" Mia wrapped an arm around Calvin's waist.

"Yes." Tony's green orbs locked in on his wife's and they were full of love and pride.

"What were some of the pitfalls in the initial phases and how did you overcome them?" Cameron asked, pulling Tony's attention back to the group.

Daron listened intently as Tony answered but also noticed Levi circling through a group of people standing near them. Marquise had not made an appearance. The six of them had a great conversation on everything from the state of the Black community to the prison system, politics, and technological advances.

"Excuse me. I'll be back in a moment," Daron stated, then leaned toward Cameron's ear, whispering, "Going to the restroom."

Cameron's gaze flickered toward Mia, she grimaced then returned her focus to the conversation as Daron slipped into the crowd. Daron quickly handled his business, but as he was washing his hands Levi entered.

"You do like your ladies beautiful." Levi leaned on the silver damask wallpaper. "I bet your Missus is good with her mouth." He smiled, placing a hand over his crotch.

"You will never know." Daron grabbed the door handle. Levi placed his palm flat on the door.

"Tell her if she needs a real man to satisfy her, I'll happily show her the only reason she prefers you is because she's never had me."

"Yet, you didn't tell her that when you had a chance." Daron chuckled, snatching the door open and heading back to the group. He was not about to play Levi's game, at least not until he was ready to completely shut him down.

CHAPTER 13

Cameron hated the feeling that everything was becoming half-truths and withheld information when it came to Daron. She promised herself that she would be patient and let Daron tell her in his own time. However, when she had to shake a tail to get to his house this was a problem that could not be ignored. After the garage incident, she gave up riding her motorcycle, switching back to the Charger.

"Did you meet the candidates?" Trenton, her computer specialist, asked.

Cameron adjusted the Bluetooth in her ears. "Alisha's trouble but Ralph might be a good fit. I especially like Tony and Kari Baltimore but they're not even under consideration."

"They should be. Solves two of Daron's problems; safety and principled leadership. That Pastor is extremely visible, has a truce in place with the criminal element in the neighborhood and Levi would be crazy to come on church grounds, talking about he owns one of those kids under Tony's care. Tony would eat him alive."

"Knowing Daron, he'll probably donate to Tony's programs but he wants a leader who has not fully tapped into their potential so that he can be hands-on in developing his vision."

"I'll check the database to see what I can find about Alisha and Ralph."

"Focus on Jake for now." She paused at the base of the driveway. "Steve's investigating them. Let's see what he finds first."

"You sure that's the only reason you have a problem with her." Trenton cleared his throat before saying. "She's a beautiful woman."

"I'm not intimidated by other women's beauty," Cameron fired back, slightly insulted that Trenton would even insinuate such a thing. "Daron's a grown-ass man. He either wants to be with me or he doesn't. I'd literally have to lock the man in his house to keep him from running into beautiful women."

"Umm, okay." Trenton was silent for a moment. "Back to your dad."

She jogged up the concrete stairs, looked over her shoulder to scan the area and went to the side of the house where she couldn't be seen from either street as Trenton gave the update on Jake Stone but nothing seemed earth-shatteringly new.

"Look into Levi Diesel for me, he reminds me a little too much of Bishop," Cameron said before disconnecting the call.

By the time she reached the front door, Daron stepped on the porch wearing slacks and a white collarless dress shirt. His gaze was intense, as though searching for answers. Her eyes roamed over his physique. He had become hyper-alert to his surroundings and that was before Levi's threat. He was taking more calls that required him to step into the privacy of his office. This was not the same man she was dealing with prior to getting that early morning call about Tracy being missing.

"Who are you hiding from, gorgeous?" Daron tugged on her cap. His woodsy cologne enveloped her as he pulled her into his well-cut arms.

"No one."

He leaned down, planting a quick kiss on her lips before stepping aside to let her in.

Cameron pulled off her cap, slipped off her shoes. She didn't want to mention the covert operation required to get to his house and not simply as a part of her normal safety habits. Since it started before Levi and the situation with Katara and Tracy were handled, something else had to be going on. "I'm going to take a shower and change real quick."

"Since we're staying in tonight." Daron gestured to the kitchen. "I picked up some Beggar's pizza and made a salad."

"I'm good with that." She stared at him "I'm just going to freshen up. Be right back."

"Meet me in the entertainment room." Daron grabbed plates, then gave a half-smile "Since this is our chill with a movie night."

She smiled back and left the room, showered and pushed all thoughts of their issues aside before heading to join him. Leaning in the threshold, Cameron watched Daron as he meticulously put salad on the plates. Cameron accepted part of the blame for the trackers. She asked him to create a legal business to purchase his security system but she had no idea his brilliant mind would create a personal security system for ladies.

"Are you coming in or are you going to continue to stand there and stare at me all night?" Daron looked back at her, lifted a plate then returned it to the coffee table.

"Don't hate on me for appreciating the view." She pushed away from the wall, moving toward him.

"Never that." He chuckled, extending his hand toward the part of the couch where she normally sat. "I'm inviting you to come a little closer to do so."

"I can do that." Cameron was really hoping she wouldn't have to give him space. She had gotten accustomed to having him in her life. However, she had to think about the main reason she closed up shop and allowed her crew to take over. What if the men who were following her, happened to see her while she was with her mother?

"How's following your dad going?" Daron picked up the remote, starting John Wick.

"Hard man to follow but he seems to be more interested in Dr. Oakley, Dr. Metra, and Dr. Sibley out of all the doctors he's visited." Cameron bit into the pizza slice, wishing she had fries instead of salad. "Trenton's looking to see what their specialties are and if we can find a common thread."

"Let me know if you need any assistance."

As they ate and watched a movie, Cameron couldn't stop staring at Daron. His eyes were on the television but he seemed lost in thought.

She picked up the remote and turned off the television. "What's going on with you?"

He polished off the portion in his mouth. "Aunt Bee's mission to unearth Troy's killer has me thinking about the past." Daron reclined until his he rested on the couch. "I'm amazed at how well my family kept things from me. I didn't realize until my mom died that for a short period people thought my dad ran Bishop's organization. That's how we ended up in Morgan Park. They weren't really known in the area. Dad took a job at the Ford plant."

Cameron cuddled into his side, recalling the stories Bishop used to tell about his partner in crime. "Your dad was Rook?"

Daron nodded.

She looked up at him, wondering if something else had prompted the reflection. "Bishop talked about him quite often."

Her cell vibrated on the table. She was surprised to see her friend, Kathleen Frost's name on the screen.

"Who is it?"

Cameron turned the screen display his way.

"Your mysterious female friend." Daron sat up, reaching for his drink. "Are you going to answer?"

She swiped, then said, "What do I owe the honor?"

"I got business in the city and thought I'd holler at you for a minute." Kathleen's voice was slightly muffled.

"Do you need me to come be your bodyguard?" Cameron always teased Kathleen for the amount of attention she drew back in the days when they worked together on a few assignments.

"I should be guarding you the way men fall at your feet," she shot back.

Cameron glanced at Daron. At the moment he was the only man she wanted and the place Cameron wanted him was definitely not at her feet. "I don't even know how you manage to be so stealthy when your ass causes tremors when you walk."

Daron's eyes widened as he cocked his head, staring at her.

"Damn you're still crazy." Kathleen chuckled. "You down to meet tonight?"

"Can I meet tonight?" Cameron stared at Daron waiting to answer until he nodded. "Yeah if you don't mind me bringing a man who's visibly shocked I have a female friend."

Kathleen chuckled. "Does he have any handsome single friends?"

"He does, but are you and Jamar still doing your off and on thing?" Cameron tucked the phone between the shoulder and ear to help Daron as he started to clear the dinner plates off the coffee table.

Kathleen didn't respond.

"I'm going to take that as a yes." Cameron made plans to meet, then laid the cell down. "Hey, if you really want to stay in, I'll call her back and arrange to meet with her another time."

Daron pulled her into his arms. "I don't want to miss out on the opportunity to see Kathleen in person. I can't ever recall Bishop mentioning her."

"Kathleen comes from a family who are talented at being undetectable," she explained, heading into the bathroom to put in the brown contacts. "Their services are high in demand."

"Is she as lethal as you?" Daron followed her, leaning in the door frame.

"Her craft is getting in and out of places undetected." Cameron watched his expressions through the mirror. "She can defend herself, she's a great shot, but she's not an assassin or gun for hire. That's her oldest brother's thing. I'm surprised that Bishop didn't warn you about the Frost family."

"I find it interesting you're giving me such a hard time about retiring when your tribe is filled with tethers to your old life. I should be the one worried, not you."

"I was never the face of any organization." Cameron put an index finger over his mouth as he opened it to speak. "Tonight is about meeting a friend, not rehashing old shit. Drinks, friendly conversation and no drama." At least she hoped, there would be no problems.

CHAPTER 14

The first face Daron noticed when they entered was Marquise with his crew sitting in the back. He selected a table that was near the wall where he had a clear view of Marquise's booth and the entrance. Cameron frowned, glancing in the direction of the men as the waitress took their order and quickly returned since they were so close to the bar.

"It's not a good thing that Levi threw down the gauntlet like that. Especially since he hasn't really done anything but popped up at the center to see me once and invite me to his restaurant." Cameron sipped the Heineken, cutting her eyes at the booth where the four men surrounding Marquise smoked their cigars. "Maybe his dislike of you is about you being back in business?"

"*Babe*, I guarantee you that is not the reason." Daron wanted to remind Cameron she had said focus on taking Levi down above all else. He glanced at Marquise and knew the last thing he needed was for him to see the two of them not getting along.

"I'm just making sure you didn't skip over the obvious choice." Cameron pursed her lips and narrowed those brown eyes as she tapped the display of her phone. Suddenly, she looked toward the door and smiled. "Maybe we should change locations."

Kathleen knocked on the table. "Am I interrupting?" Her black hat pulled low on her face.

Daron stood, pulling out a chair for their guest. "Not at all."

"Daron, Kathleen." Cameron introduced the two, then waved the waitress over.

"Nice to meet you."

Daron's phone chimed. He glanced at the display and decided maybe Cameron needed some time alone with her friend. "This is Steve. I probably should take this."

"Okay."

Daron placed a kiss on Cameron's forehead before slowly stepping away.

"That's his way of giving us a few minutes to catch up," Cameron said, as Daron moved toward the door, positioning himself so his gaze fell to Marquise.

"Hey, I'm out with Cam and one of her girlfriends, I'll have to call you back." Daron slipped out the door, not wanting Cameron to see the exchange between him and Marquise.

"What?" Steve's voice raised an octave.

Marquise rose from his seat, headed Daron's way but changed direction.

"I have to go," Daron said as Marquise stood near the section of the bar closest to Kathleen and Cameron. He reentered, crossing the tile with long strides.

"Miss Thing here tells me you have lots of single friends," Kathleen said as Daron lowered himself into a chair.

"I have a decent amount." Daron smiled, taking this opportunity to move to a different location. "How about we go to another bar and the guys meet us there?"

"I'm good with that." Kathleen smiled, sipping her beer.

Cameron laughed but her focus went to Daron, then Kathleen. "You would be. Miss Troublemaker."

"Let me see who's available, then we'll select a new spot." Daron sent out a few texts.

"I hope you don't mind waiting until my wings arrive." Kathleen looked around for the waitress.

"Not at all," Daron replied, even though he was eager to be somewhere he could relax and enjoy getting to know Kathleen and learn about the dynamics of the two women's friendship.

They laughed and talked as Kathleen ate the wings that had been slathered in hot sauce. Daron's phone vibrated. He'd finally received a confirmation reserving a VIP section of an establishment owned by his friend, Zack Shaw.

His gaze was glued to the door, following the group of men that entered.

Cameron rested her hand on his thigh. "Do we have a problem?"

"I hope not," Daron replied as Marquise and his men approached the table.

"Two beautiful ladies with a man who has the intellect of a wad of gum on the bottom of a shoe." Marquise claimed the empty seat next to Daron.

"Now that you've insulted me, you can leave and allow me to finish enjoying my evening." Daron definitely didn't want to get into an argument with Marquise and have him mention The Castle.

"Ladies enjoy his company while you can. If he doesn't make the right choices over the next few weeks, I'll do what most people do with scum, dispose of it." Marquise rose from the wooden table. "Stay away from my boy, he has the potential to do big things in my organization."

Daron didn't know whether he was referring to Amarion or Reese. "I've had enough of these intimidation tactics from a man who's always hiding behind his bodyguards."

"Maybe you want to take this conversation outside." Marquise nodded to the door. "Maybe I'll stop wasting time and take you out of the game altogether and permanently end any future conversations."

Cameron angled her cell, snapping a few pictures. One of Marquise's goons advanced toward Daron. Both women shifted their chair and Daron placed his hand on Cameron's shoulder.

Marquise snapped his fingers, drawing the attention of the muscled man leaning on the wall near the entrance. He pushed the door open enough so Daron could see Amarion looking confused as he stood outside next to one of Marquise's goons. Probably unaware that a gun was being aimed at his back as Marquise held up an index finger. "Oh, I haven't even gotten started yet. When I do, you'll be willing to handle business any way I see fit."

Daron activated the device to prevent cameras from recording, then snaked his arm around Marquise's neck in a chokehold. He stuck the Beretta into Marquise's side. "I'm not scared of anyone who threatens children," Daron whispered in his ear, as the two goons surged forward.

Kathleen and Cameron got to their feet with their weapons in their hands, daring his goons to keep advancing. Patrons' heads whipped around, watching the altercation.

"Be warned, if anything happens to him and I mean even a scratch." He squeezed Marquise's neck tightly, staring at the man holding the gun on Amarion. "I'll have no problem being the sledgehammer that crushes you."

Marquise's face was flaming red as he waved off the shooter. Daron released his neck but kept the Beretta stuck in his side because one thing he was not, was a fool.

CHAPTER 15

Last night, Daron was able to salvage the rest of the evening once they changed venues. Not enough to prevent a heated discussion on the way home or Cameron from sleeping in the guest bedroom. He worked off the frustration by making alterations to an invention for Calvin's top-secret project. He still couldn't believe he'd thrown a lit match on a relationship that was already doused with gasoline. It pissed him off that Cameron tossed back the house key, officially ending the pursuit of a lasting union without hesitation. He flashed back to how the morning started.

Daron sipped his coffee, trying to compensate for only getting an hour of sleep. He retrieved the extra set of keys as Cameron took long strides toward the island. "Was last night's incident about Amarion and the program?"

"I can't even get a good morning." Daron frowned, inhaling deeply.

"So, is that a yes?"

His cell rang and when he answered he received an evil glare from Cameron. "Hey, Steve."

"Brandi interrupted Roger's poker night and turned over tables, literally," Steve said. The shock carried in his voice.

"Is she hurt?" Daron stared at Cameron, who looked like she was seconds from ripping the cell from his hands.

"Nope. It seems Brandi had as many friends in the room as Roger did."

Daron ended the call and took a sip of coffee. "I have a long day ahead of me. If you're not ready to trust me and stop using my past against me, leave the keys with Steve when you see him at the gym." Daron sat the mug down then placed the house keys in her hands. "If you can, I'll see you tonight."

"No need." Cameron tossed the keys to him. She shot him a look that dropped the temperature in the room ten degrees below zero. "Clearly, it's time for us to go our separate ways." Her lips tightened as her eyes threw daggers at him for a moment before she headed to the door.

He couldn't dwell on that at the moment. If he wanted a chance at getting his relationship with Cameron back on the right path, he needed to tackle The Castle problem. He had no intention of begging her to come back. It's not like he didn't have a clue what type of woman he was dealing with from the get-go, which was why he was using a firm but gentle approach with her. Unfortunately, Daron didn't have that in him at the start of the day. With Cameron, the absence wouldn't make the heart grow fonder. It would only solidify the distance between them. He would have a small window of time to put a plan in place that maneuvered her back into his life before he found himself on the outskirts of hers, along with her father who had made the unforgivable mistake of leaving her in jail.

Daron was already in the process of gathering intel to bring Marquise to his knees. If he were anything like his godfather, his people were looking for the weakest link to intimidate into doing it their way.

He slid the silver cufflinks on, partially wanting to miss this event but it was an opportunity to see Ralph in action. Cameron was supposed to attend but then this morning happened. He became frustrated and upset all over again that she walked away so easily. He exited the house and hopped in the Porsche.

First, he had to bring Marquise to justice, which would be a challenge since he had others committing the crime.

As he drove, his thoughts were on what had transpired since getting involved with The Castle. Cameron had been right about him being much busier. He parked and entered the school's gym, today he had volunteered to help with the etiquette event. Alisha's dark-brown skin glowed under the stage lighting. He wasn't aware that she was participating, otherwise he would have sent Pedro in his place.

Alisha's face seemed fuller as she smiled. Her wavy black hair fell over her face as she adjusted the microphone. He glanced at the designer suit that complimented her figure. *Red must be her favorite color.* She grabbed something off the podium and headed straight for him.

"Hey, handsome," she purred. "Great seeing you again. Let me put you to work. Would you mind helping me set the table?"

"Not at all." Daron slid his phone into his jacket. "That's what I'm here for."

She gave him a quick embrace then pointed him in Ralph's direction. Volunteering gave him an opportunity to see how he worked and handled problems.

"It's a great thing you're doing here." Daron took one of the tables that Ralph had retrieved from the closet and rested it on the wall.

"One of these programs saved my life." He locked up the closet and dropped the key into his top pocket. "I'm just giving back, hoping it will do the same for someone else.

"How many volunteers do you normally have?"

"Five to ten depending on the event." Ralph lifted a table off the wall. "Alisha has been a big help tonight since my go-to person is sick."

Daron rolled the table next to him. "Do you have regular volunteers?"

"Workers from similar programs are usually my normal volunteers. The other volunteers are parents." Ralph sat the table near a taped X on the floor, then pointed for Daron to do the same at another black taped X. "Some parents want to learn as their child learns. Others are parents who just want to help out."

The last few tables were quickly set up to match the others. Seconds later, the kids were rushing in for the event. Etiquette experts stood at the podium while two adults sat at each table to assist the kids. Alisha's energy and the kids' excitement were contagious. Hard to stay solemn with the positive vibes circling around him. Alisha kept the kids entertained with games and stories in between speakers.

The function was over in what felt like a heartbeat. Daron noticed Ralph talking to a red-haired man in a tan linen suit who hadn't shown up until they were cleaning. *Maybe he's a parent.* Ralph pointed inside the room where there were only three volunteers left, including himself. The linen suit left. Daron could only assume that the person he was looking for wasn't there.

"I wish I had something like this when I was growing up," Alisha said as she gathered up the silk flower centerpiece and placed it in a box.

Daron removed the tablecloth, stuffed it in the laundry bag and trailed her to the next table. "I don't see it taking you long to catch on."

She shifted the box on her hip. "I followed whatever everyone else did."

"That's why we're here tonight so they won't have the same experience." Daron followed her to the corner where the volunteers were stacking all the items.

"Yes, the girls from my program were at the table with Ralph." She placed the box down on the stack. "They're hoping to use what they learned tonight at the Art & Jewelry Gala since two of the girls will be selected to attend."

"What is that?" Daron caught the box as it almost tipped over and returned it neatly on top of the pile.

"An auction that raises money for nonprofits. The more money raised, the more organizations can be helped."

"I assume it's a big deal."

"It is. Each artist creates a piece of jewelry that speaks to whatever is painted on the canvas." Alisha smiled, shoulders lifted slightly in her excitement. "Two organizations are randomly assigned to each set. And will split the proceeds."

"Some pairings will bring in more money?"

"Yes. One pairing is already at a million in the silent online auction. While there's a cap on how much a single organization can receive, the additional money goes into a fund to sponsor field trips and speakers.

Whatever's left by the end of the school year ..." She bent over, picked up a few napkins that had fallen to the floor, then tossed them in the trash. "... They give out scholarships to kids in the program who are graduating and going into college."

Daron walked toward another table. "That's great."

"I didn't understand how much my mom helped and protected me until she died when I was in grammar school." Alisha ran her fingers through her hair. "I've had to make a lot of hard choices to survive, some I wasn't proud of."

"So, you really understand these girls."

"My dad believed in me earning my keep once my mother was gone. Things changed a bit when he finally settled down again with one woman but she discovered something she didn't like about him and left us." Alisha looked over his shoulder. Her eyes widened and the centerpiece she'd just grabbed wobbled in her hand.

Daron glanced back to see what had stolen her focus.

Alisha seemed to stare through the door. "Could you help Ralph get the last few tables out?" She placed the centerpiece in the box then looked at the older man struggling to roll out a table.

"Sure." Daron wondered what she had actually seen that shook her. Because it definitely wasn't Ralph.

"Thanks for your help," Ralph held open the closet door. "A lot of people like to help set up but not break down. That is, unless food is involved."

Daron placed the last table into the closet when he noticed a stocky man about five-nine with red hair and light blue eyes approach Alisha. He'd seen him earlier talking with Ralph as well.

He walked over to collect the jacket he'd laid over one of the plastic chairs lining the hall. "You're welcome."

His eyes were on Alisha and the man, who she seemed to be having a disagreement with. Alisha gave the man a withering look before reaching around him to grab her purse off the chair and leaving with the man trailing her.

"Alisha's a sweetheart. Always pitching in to help." Ralph scanned the hallway, then he peeked into the gym. "Have you seen her? She didn't say goodnight."

"She just left."

"That's odd." Ralph shrugged. "Oh well, I'll catch up with her later to see how she thought it went."

"I'll make sure to sign up for the next one." Daron slid on the suit jacket and quickly headed out the door to make sure Alisha had made it to her car alright.

When he entered the parking lot, the words 'I'm in too deep' caught his attention. A group of men congregated near the corner.

Alisha snatched her arm away from the red-haired man and opened the door to an Infiniti Q50. "Don't touch me."

"You know what I want." He yanked her toward him.

"Let me go." Alisha struggled to get out of his hold.

"Alisha is everything okay?" Daron called out as he approached.

"No. I keep telling him I'm not interested."

"This does not concern you." The linen suit snarled something at Alisha that Daron couldn't hear as she tugged against him. The handle of his gun peeked out from under his waistband.

"If she's told you to leave her alone and you don't, then it becomes my business." Daron was hoping he'd walk away from getting into an altercation that could bring the police, which wasn't ideal but he also couldn't allow Alisha to be manhandled.

"Stick to sitting behind the desk." He released Alisha and stepped forward.

Daron buttoned his jacket since he wasn't sure the shirt Cameron gifted him had Kevlar in it. "Don't let the suit fool you."

"Oh, you're a corporate thug." He chuckled, scanning the streets as though expecting backup. "Excuse me but I'll serve your ass to you and have you begging to return to the safety of your little office."

"You intimidate women," Daron said, as Alisha shifted closer to the champagne Infiniti. "And I'm supposed to be scared of you?"

A thin, bearded fellow with dirty-brown hair and a serious snarl rushed their way.

"This ain't none of your business." The red-haired man glared at Alisha, yanking her back to him. "This conversation isn't over, Miss Thing."

The thin man made it to them, his eyes lasered on Alisha's cleavage. "Bobby, I heard you were looking for me."

The red-haired guy stepped away from Alisha. "Are you a fool?"

Daron noticed a car jutted off the side road, almost getting hit as the window lowered and a glint of light shimmered off the weapon.

"Get down," Daron yelled, yanking Alisha while reaching for the Beretta as he moved behind the black sedan to his left.

The slim guy wasn't quick enough. His body jerked as a bullet ripped through his shoulder and the blood splattered on Alisha. She screamed as the bullets hit her car. The red-haired man swiveled in the direction of the vehicle driving by, firing back as he moved toward a Lexus. He slid behind the wheel of the car, tires screeched as the vehicle peeled away.

Daron moved toward the injured man, realizing he'd been hit twice, and applied pressure to his torso. He called to Alisha, who stood trembling near the car with dark stain splatters on her dress. "Were you hit?"

She shook her head.

"Call 911."

With shaky hands, Alisha retrieved her cell and made the call. The man on the ground moaned. His breathing was shallow as he touched the wound on his shoulder then stared at his bloody hand. "I shouldn't have worked with ..."

"The police and ambulance are on their way," Alisha announced, kneeling to use her scarf to apply pressure to the shoulder wound.

His eyes rolled back in his head and seconds later, he passed out.

Ralph ran out of the center toward them.

"Is he still alive?" Ralph shifted Alisha out the way as the sirens in the distance got closer.

"Yes." Hand in his pocket, Daron pressed the button for the device to prevent cell phones from recording the incident.

Alisha pressed herself against the Infiniti, glued to the driver's side.

The emergency vehicle pulled up and a couple of EMTs rushed to them.

Ralph and Daron stepped back to allow paramedics to take over.

Daron turned to Alisha, who threw herself into his arms. "You okay?"

"I am now." She pressed her breasts into his chest as she wrapped her arms around him, then rested her head on his chest. She looked up, arms still wrapped around him. "Thank you."

Daron extracted himself from her hold as the police in their dark-blue uniforms approached. Her chest moved rapidly, as if she had been holding her breath and just started to breathe. A blond stocky police officer requested that Daron move to one side as another one moved Alisha in the other direction. The officers weren't slick. They were separating them to take their statements. People started gathering behind the caution tape with phones attempting to capture the aftermath. Daron quickly stood against the wall and out of most of the phones' range then he hit the button to allow video recording. As the injured man was loaded into the ambulance; the police placed yellow numbered markers around the lot and took crime scene pictures.

The process felt like it took hours. Ralph let them back into the gym to clean up a bit. Daron noticed as they exited the building that Alisha's gaze focused on a point across the street.

"Do you want me to give you a ride home?" Daron wondered how many bullets had hit her car, which was still trapped within the crime scene.

She wrapped both arms around herself. "If you don't mind."

Daron opened the door and she slid into the passenger seat, looking at him with a hint of desire in her eyes. She tugged on her skirt that had risen up her thigh and slowly licked her lips.

"Not at all." Daron closed the door, unable to shake the feeling that there was more to the situation than he was seeing.

She gave him an address near Hyde Park. The first few minutes of the short journey were made in silence as he reflected on the evening. *Were they actually shooting at the man harassing Alisha?*

Alisha had given him some kind of feeling when they first met but he wrote it off once he discovered she was attracted to him. Was Alisha in trouble?

"This isn't how I expected the night to end." Alisha lifted her trembling hands as Daron held the Porsche door open.

Alisha reached into her purse which emitted a tinkling sound as she retrieved her keys.

Daron seized the keys from her unsteady hand and unlocked the door.

"Let me at least get you some coffee," Alisha implored as she accepted the keys back.

"It's been a long night." Daron turned, heading to the Porsche.

Alisha grabbed his bicep. "I insist. I have to-go cups. Come on. Let me at least do that for you."

Maybe he'd find out what happened between her and her assailant before he'd arrived. "Sure."

He stepped into her living room, an elegant space with contemporary upscale decor.

Alisha immediately washed her hands and put on the coffee. "I'll be right back."

Daron's thoughts were on the incident, hoping Cameron's brothers didn't catch wind of it and connect it to him before he had a chance to make things right with their sister. The Stone brothers definitely didn't want him with their sister and would surely tell her. The more he thought about what Cameron had been through because of him in recent weeks, he somewhat understood her walking away even though he had a huge issue with the swift execution.

"Sorry I took so long," Alisha said, as she returned to the kitchen wearing a black silk robe that was mere inches below her ass.

If Daron wasn't with Cameron, the night may have ended very differently. The only thing he wanted from Alisha was to find out what kind of trouble she had gotten herself into and see if he could assist in resolving her problem.

CHAPTER 16

"I don't like this last-minute change to the meeting." Daron located a satellite image of the new building, then forwarded it to their security team. He returned the tablet to the special pocket in his jacket. The group wanted to convince Calvin they could benefit greatly from the use of the device that made the wearer invisible to the naked eye, which they called The Emperor's Suit, since Calvin hadn't made the final decision who would gain the contract to use The Suit for at least a year, with the option to renew for another three years.

"Umm, what's with the fan?" Calvin asked, looking at the metal fan lying near Daron's cell phone on the console. "It's not very unisex."

"It's a prototype shield designed for a woman." Daron picked up two items, slipping his cell into his pocket. He opened the fan and made a complete circle. When the metal bars clicked together, the second layer of metal blades popped out to complete the shield. "I don't know what made me grab it."

"Nice." Calvin touched the metal of the shield. "I will have to take a closer look after the meeting." He maneuvered a BMW X3 out of the parking lot of the original location where they were scheduled to talk with a special operations task force. "Once you come up with a more unisex design, I can add cloaking. It could be one of The Suit's accessories."

"Unfortunately, men don't carry as many items as women, so I'm still brainstorming items I can convert." Daron pressed the buttons along the handle to retract the second layer, then closed the fan and put it in his pocket.

"Thanks for the detail. While security is what Mia does, I hate the idea of her standing outside conference rooms and my lab when I'm working," Calvin said, while he weaved through the slow traffic on the street as he made his way toward Museum of Science and Industry to get on to Lake Shore drive.

"I told Mia not to worry. Your team will be all men, except when I'm present to make sure you don't get in trouble." Daron looked at Calvin as he stopped at the light and saw the man's grimace. "We know what happened with the last female working a detail for you."

Mia had been hired to protect Calvin and his invention and she'd barely been able to keep him alive with so many people trying to kill him.

"Funny Kincaid. Real funny." Calvin chuckled, then his facial expression became serious as the light turned green. He turned his attention to the road. "Why didn't you have Cam protect me?"

"She's not on my payroll." Between the Katara-Tracy situation and his suddenly having a busy schedule, his relationship with Cameron had been as bi-polar as Chicago's seasons. One minute they were in the middle of a polar vortex and the next in a heatwave. He wondered if Cameron mentioned to Mia that they weren't together at the moment.

"How is the search going for a director to head your youth program?" Calvin asked as the BMW inched forward in the thick traffic as they passed by the Shedd Aquarium.

"We've narrowed the list to two." Daron wanted to have an idea who the individuals were before he even approached them with the proposal. He gazed out of the window, watching as one of the two security vehicles accompanying them zoomed ahead.

Calvin honked at a yellow cab and barely missed hitting the BMW as it squeezed in front of him.

The cool summer air blew into the truck as Daron watched to make sure his team was the only people following them.

"How's it going, you being a part of The Castle?" Calvin asked, something he did regularly.

"Keeping me busy. But don't worry, we'll get the trackers in all The Suits," Daron answered as Calvin finally pulled into the parking lot of the new location. He had Nicco beta testing The Suits with trackers to transport Khalil from The Castle.

A few seconds later, Linc pulled in beside him. Linc, who was six foot seven, bearded with a muscular form, was naturally intimidating to most. "Crystal's heading the B team and will check the back entrance. Anita and Bryson will stay with you and Calvin," Linc ordered, walking toward the door. "Roc you're with me."

"Send the drone in first," Daron instructed as Anita Roseboro stood watching the parking lot entrance and Bryson scanned the ground. Linc, along with the remaining man on the team, entered the building.

Daron launched another drone to check the rooftop.

"Man, if it wasn't for my previous experience with people chasing Mia and me down for The Suits, I probably would've thought this was overkill." Calvin shifted the gold bracelet on his wrist.

"At least there's no snipers." Daron waited for Linc and Crystal to give the all-clear.

"Heading to the conference room. We checked the lobby, so you can come in now," Linc said.

Daron adjusted the device in his ear as Bryson moved toward the door. "We're going in."

Calvin followed Daron as Anita brought up the rear.

Crystal Baltimore came on the com line. "The back is secure. No cars, and rear doors are locked. Doubling back your way."

Daron made a mental note to ask after the meeting if she was related to Tony. They entered the building through two sets of doors and crept down a long hall to a large waiting area set up with a leather couch and two matching seats. Light rock played through the speaker system. The place gave off eerie vibes.

Linc could be seen at the end of the hallway with Roc, a waif of a woman wearing a beige dress that looked two sizes too big. "The conference room has been swept but I think you should reschedule."

"Sorry Calvin," Daron said. He had a bad feeling about this too, and didn't need to hear Linc's reason for the decision. He noticed both men already had their hands hovering over their weapons as if they were expecting trouble at any moment.

"I trust your team." Calvin retrieved the BMW keys from his pocket. "Did you tell the people in the conference?"

"No one was there," Linc replied, with a hand close to his weapon.

Daron immediately tapped Anita on the shoulder. "You drive Calvin. I'll ride with Linc."

Linc was just beyond two steel doors that were propped open when Crystal called out. "Get out now. Several additional heat signatures are rising from the floor."

Bryson drew his weapon as Linc shot down the hallway at the men.

"They're coming up a hidden tunnel in the floor." Linc grabbed the young lady as he and Roc crossed the threshold. Linc pushed the door closed seconds before men with automatic weapons entered off the side hallway.

Daron stepped out firing, between Linc and Roc as the door opened. Anita drew her weapon as she moved Calvin back toward the front entrance.

"I'm only a temp. I didn't sign up for this." The terrified assistant scrambled toward the wooden desk. Linc and Roc took cover behind the wall near the reception area.

Daron shot a look at Calvin, "Turn on your suit."

"That doesn't do the rest of you any good," Calvin countered.

"You're the only client here." Daron pulled out a pair of glasses from his inner pocket and handed it to Anita, so that she could see Calvin when the cloaking property was activated. "Make sure he doesn't get shot."

They raced down the long hallway to the outer door as gunfire filled the area behind Daron. Across the way, Linc had taken off his jacket and pulled out the compact automatic weapon.

"Go," Linc yelled as he fired so Roc and the young lady raced toward Daron.

"Get her to safety," Daron ordered as Roc paused near him, releasing the woman. "Tell her to ditch the heels."

Daron maneuvered the drone into the hall. Four men with bulletproof vests were tucked behind the steel doors leading to the conference room.

"Boss, go," Linc commanded.

"Crystal, location?" Daron refused to leave Linc in this by himself.

"We just made it to the front of the building," she replied, the sound of a vehicle coming to a screeching halt echoed in the background. "You should see us soon."

Daron pulled out the fan, opened the shield, then stepped in the passageway firing shots as Linc reloaded the clip. One man was hit in the leg as the other three advanced. Daron clipped another one in the arm. Several bullets hit the shield before he was forced to take cover. Crystal, with two others, ran toward the action.

"Linc," Daron slid the shield to him. "Take cover behind the desk," he instructed, snatching open the nearest door then flattening himself against the wall. He nodded for Bryson to do the same. "Crystal. Fire."

Three assailants stepped in front of the reception desk moments before bullets penetrated the glass behind it, sending shards in all directions. Two men scattered, one returned fire, hitting one of Daron's people. Linc slammed the shield on the back of the shooter's head. They tussled but it didn't take long for Linc to subdue him. Crystal and Bryson raced after the two attackers. Daron checked on the drone feed and the other two men were lifting a panel in a floor down the other hall seconds before his team reached them.

"Crystal don't follow. Just secure the area." Daron didn't know what would be waiting for them in those tunnels. He walked over to the injured man leaning against the wall. "How bad is it?"

"Just a graze," the man grimaced, holding the bloody wound.

The front entrance flew open. Daron swung his gun up at three men, two of whom looked like they were military.

"I see we're late to the party," the one with a dark-blue suit and crew cut said.

They were the men Calvin and he were actually supposed to meet. They received the meeting notification but had the time pegged for thirty-minutes later.

Sirens filled the parking lot. A few police officers entered the building, swept the space then secured it as a crowd gathered outside. The remaining officers began questioning Daron's team on what occurred. Calvin had been taken somewhere safe by Anita and had only returned to give his statement. Bryson rode to the hospital with the injured team member.

"I'm glad no one died today," Calvin declared as they headed to the BMW. following Anita who slid behind the wheel.

A man who appeared to be homeless lingering among the onlookers caught Daron's eye. His gaze was too focused on the three of them. Before Daron could approach him, the man disappeared into the crowd. "Get in the car now."

The homeless man reappeared in the distance behind two police officers as they opened the truck's doors. Daron went for the gun but hesitated.

The cops would take him out, not realizing he was aiming for the man between them. Daron reached for the fan to create a shield but realized Linc still had it. He pushed Calvin against the BMW as the homeless guy pointed a gun at Daron, firing off four shots.

"No," Calvin yelled as Daron's body slammed against the door's inner paneling.

Screams filled the air.

The officers swiveled around, bolting after the shooter and fighting to make their way through the chaos of scattering onlookers.

Daron's chest, abs, and shoulder felt as if he'd been hit with a sledgehammer and it took him a moment to catch his breath.

"What the hell?" Calvin patted Daron's upper body. His eyes were wide with horror.

"A gift from Cam," Daron muttered, touching the bullet still lodged in the center of his chest.

Calvin pulled Daron upright. "Tell her I'm going to need her tailor's name until I figure out how to make my own device bulletproof."

Linc jogged over. "Sorry man. Saw him but he was a professional. He aligned himself so I couldn't take the shot."

Daron slowly slid into the passenger seat. "At this point, I just want to know who has some painkillers."

***

Marquise came way too close.

The Porsche stopped at the red light and Daron peered down his shirt at the bruise. Linc insisted on following him since Daron refused to let anyone drive him once he returned to the car. Daron was a few minutes away from home when a call came through. At first. he thought it was the doctor who he'd asked to meet him at the house. The screen displayed Reese's name, instead.

"Levi and his men are scouring the streets gunning for Cedric." Reese's voice sounded muffled.

"Get somewhere safe and I'll find him before they do," Daron said, changing directions.

As Daron reached the corner of the block with the kickback house, two muscular men in suits were moving about with guns boldly in their hands. He sped off, heading toward Cedric's uncle's house first with Linc on his tail. He'd be smart enough not to go home.

Linc's number appeared on the screen. Daron grimaced as he tapped the display to answer.

"Boss, what's going on?"

"Levi's looking for one of my boys," Daron replied, whipping onto Cedric's block.

As Daron neared his house, he saw Cedric sprinting up the stairs with Levi and two thugs on his tail. The front door closed behind Cedric but Levi slammed a foot into the wood and flung it open.

"Dammit." Daron hopped out of the car and pain shot through him, causing him to cringe. He caught a glimpse of Cedric bolting out the backyard into the alley.

Daron jumped back in and shot off up the block and around the corner, cutting down the alley. He hit the horn to keep Cedric from sprinting through to another house then lowered the window. Linc hit the brakes behind him. "Cedric!"

Cedric glanced back, changed course, raced to the passenger side and jumped in. Daron peeled off with Linc pausing at the alley, probably to ensure Levi couldn't get a shot off.

It looks like I'll be switching cars again.

Daron glanced in the rearview to see Levi standing just beyond Linc's vehicle. He slammed his fist into the guy next to him.

"Mr. Dee when I say I'm glad to see you …" Cedric buckled up, then rested his head on the seat. His breathing was heavy in the silence.

Daron maneuvered toward a safe house in Beverly. "Why was Levi chasing you?"

"He wanted to use my computer skills to track down your real address." Cedric lifted his arms, showing the bruising where he'd been restrained. "I was able to get away."

CHAPTER 17

Cameron couldn't believe Daron had been shot yesterday. Then again, she could. When she found out, the first thing she did was to place an expedited order for an item that would increase his chances of surviving another incident of that nature. She passed the package to Steve, when he arrived at the gym, to deliver to Daron.

"Are you and Daron okay?" Kathleen's voice switched from her earpiece to the car as Cameron started the engine.

She checked her surroundings then pulled out of the parking spacing. "Why do you ask?"

"I was handling some business near Hyde Park and saw him escorting a woman into a house," Kathleen explained.

Alisha. Cameron knew immediately before her chime came with a picture text from Kathleen. *I guess I'm the only one struggling with the separation.* She pulled over to the side to check the message. "Who in the hell is following me?"

She noticed a Mitsubishi Eclipse that had taken every turn with her the moment she left her self-defense class parked several feet behind her. "I'm going to have to holler at you later. It seems I have more pressing issues to deal with."

"Text me when the problem is handled," Kathleen said before disconnecting the line.

No way Cameron was leading them back to her house. She drove down Longwood toward 115th, tempted to go into the police station. Yet there was no guarantee they wouldn't wait for her to come out. She opted for handling the problem instead.

Cameron drove to the Morgan Park High School's track parking on the side street. She retrieved a shoulder holster out of the glove compartment and slid it over her arms then secured a weapon in each slot. Next, she grabbed her jacket, sliding it on and tucking her gold wand in one pocket.

Stepping out of the Charger, she walked directly to the car and rapped her knuckles on the window.

It slowly lowered.

"I don't appreciate being trailed."

"We don't appreciate your man recruiting our boys." The driver casually rested his arm on the window. "They have business they need to handle."

Cameron's gaze went to the light-brown, stocky man who stepped out of the passenger side. "Dude, stay in the car," she warned.

"I have no problem sending a message to him through you," he replied, tugging at his sagging grey pants.

"I'd like to see you try." She pulled out the wand and released the blade in the driver's neck. "You weren't man enough to take your issue to Daron, so you were coming for me?"

"Mark. Take her down," the driver screeched, struggling to move as his partner rounded the bumper.

Cameron jammed metal into the man's shoulder. "Nobody told you to move."

"Oh, so you are *that* girl. Ms. Self-Defense." Mark snickered, pulling out a knife of his own.

"No, I'm *that woman*." She yanked the blade out, slammed the wand against the driver's neck leaving him gasping for air.

In a swift move, she extended the wand to full staff and smashed it over Mark's arm as he approached, then jammed it into the side of his face. His eyes widen with disbelief, surprised by the sudden assault. Cameron caught movement behind her.

A pale man, who looked like he had swallowed two refrigerators whole, left a car several feet away and rushed toward her.

Cameron turned away, kicked the man in the chest and hit what felt like a brick wall. He caught her ankle before her foot made contact with the ground.

"You got moves." He yanked her toward him.

She bounced up kicking him in the side of the head. "Yep," she sneered, following up with two whacks from the wand, which forced him to release her leg. He threw a hard punch into her abs, sending her stumbling.

Mark leaned back on the hood watching as she fought the newcomer. The giant ducked under one of her swings, grabbing Cameron by the waist and squeezing.

Her guns bit into her sides, so she struck him several times across the back but it was getting harder to breathe. She retracted the wand, snatched a bead off her bracelet and stuck him in the back, then repeated her action, knowing it would take too long for the drug to kick in.

She stabbed the blade in his shoulder.

He screamed, loosening his grip but still didn't release her. The giant swayed.

Cameron kneed him in the groin.

The drug finally kicked in and he dropped to the ground.

Mark hopped up off the car as she turned her focus on him.

Cameron punched him in the face and slammed his body against the hood. She slid the wand into her waistband and whipped out the gun, jamming it against his temple. "Do you want to die today?"

She then pointed the gun at the driver, who tried to open the door. "I'm not afraid to pull the trigger."

He slid back into the seat, holding his hands up.

"Miss, are these guys harassing you?" An older, buff male raced up the sidewalk.

Cameron slid her gun into the holster. "I got it handled."

She released Mark, who quickly maneuvered to the giant. Seconds later. he struggled to lift the big guy into the back seat.

"Just a misunderstanding," Mark grunted, pushed the guy in, then rushed around to the passenger seat.

Cameron moved back after properly thanking her good Samaritan, who made sure she made it safely to the Charger. She lowered the window, prepared for them to try something. The Eclipse slowed as it inched up alongside her. Mark extended his middle finger. She lifted the Ruger, shot at the perfect angle taking the digit out. The bullet lodged in the dashboard.

He let out a string of unintelligible words, staring in disbelief at his bloody hand. Then he screamed, "You bitch, I—"

This time she aimed the Ruger toward his head. The Eclipse shot off down the street. She pulled out, driving back toward 115th. What blew her mind was that she left a dangerous business only to get attacked more now than she had been in all the years she worked for Bishop. What did they mean Daron was recruiting *their* boys? Was he really using the program as a way to find a new staff?

Unbelievable. But to be honest, it would be a perfect front. She could see Bishop doing something like that. She hadn't thought Daron was the type, but since she was certain he was hiding something, maybe this was that "thing".

You're not seeing each other anymore. Remember?

Once the self-defense sessions ended, she'd stay out of the Morgan Park area for a while. Daron was bringing the kind of heat that could get her burned.

Her cell rang interrupting her pondering. She pressed the answer button on the steering wheel.

"Hey, baby girl," Trenton's voice boomed through the vehicle.

"What's up?" Cameron pulled off, but scanned the streets for trouble.

"Why is your dad visiting all these doctors? Now he's in a hospital parking lot this time." Trenton's voice went to a whisper as if he was standing near Jake. "Something's up."

"Why are you talking so softly?" Cameron said, chuckling.

"The way your father is looking around the parking lot, I'm scared to be too loud. That man has supersonic hearing."

"Before we get my mom worried, I need you to cross-reference these doctors he's with to any latest news in the media and go back a couple of years." Cameron drove by Daron's house searching for suspicious vehicles or for the crew that attacked her.

"If there isn't a link, then what are you going to say to your mom?"

She slowed to a crawl but didn't see anything out of the ordinary. "The truth. We know he's visiting doctors but we can't confirm the reason he's tracking these people down."

"Do you want me to stay with him?"

"Where are you?" she asked as she turned and drove down the hill before maneuvering onto Longwood Avenue.

"Little Company of Mary."

"I'm not too far from there. I'm heading your way." Cameron did another check in the mirror since she hadn't seen the giant's vehicle following earlier.

"Hey, before you parted ways, did Daron mention The Castle membership Bishop left him?" Trenton asked, still in a low tone.

She filtered through their past conversations. "No."

Trenton gave her more information on The Castle. While she was hurt that Daron hadn't told her, she wasn't surprised. She was trying to give him a little time with everything that was going on. Now the idea that this Castle was filled with mob bosses, thieves, and dirty politicians was more important to him than their relationship, didn't sit well with her. What also pissed her off was that she'd told Trenton to hold off on digging into Daron's sudden secretiveness.

Maybe things are working out as they should.

Cameron dropped her guard a little more every time she and Daron were together. The separation would have been twenty times harder if she continued getting to know him.

"Let's focus on Jake," Cameron said, trying not to think about Daron or this new Castle business.

"I decided to put these physicians' names into the database to see if it would connect the dots that were missing. The system gave me a notice about The Castle. I also discovered that while I was out of the country, it was sending information to someone."

"What do you mean someone?" She drove straight down to 99th cutting across California Avenue to avoid most of the traffic jam on 95th Street.

"That's exactly my question. I'll have to hack the system to find out."

"Didn't you create that database?"

"This is Bishop we're talking about," he huffed. "I don't expect it will be easy."

"Send me what you have on Daron's membership and I'll see you soon." Cameron needed to focus on following Jake. Her mother's instinct might be valid. She probably needed to make another visit to her mother to sneak into Jake's home office and do another search.

She nodded at Trenton as he drove off, then shot Kathleen a quick text.

Jake stepped out of his sedan but swiftly got back inside. Whoever he was looking for must have come out. A tall, green-eyed man with a white lab coat and a shorter stocky man with dark hair, wearing a light brown suit, stood to one side of the doors talking until a black sedan pulled up and the shorter man got in.

Keeping a safe distance, she trailed Jake as he followed the stocky man to his destination. Jake exited the vehicle, staying out of the man's line of sight as he walked toward the building's entrance. He snapped a picture with a cell as he continued past the venue then doubled back to his sedan. Once he drove off, she slipped out of the driver's seat to see where the man, she assumed was a doctor, had gone.

Cameron checked for cameras before nearing the storefront building. As she approached the glass window, she noticed Alisha standing close to Daron as they spoke with a salt-and-pepper haired man. The doctor Jake had been following shook the older man's hand.

She snapped a photo.

Alisha slid her arm around Daron's waist as they moved in for a group picture. The woman couldn't seem to keep her hands off Daron, either patting his arms or touching his back as they looked at something. The way she was gazing at Daron with lust in her eyes, there was no doubt that she wanted them to be more than business associates. Cameron couldn't help but feel a sharp tinge of emotion. She missed Daron, but there was no future for them anyway. Recent events indicated he hadn't really left the criminal life behind. Anything tied to Bishop could never be a good thing.

The crowd dispersed, but the doctor stood off to the side staring at Daron and Alisha.

Cameron wondered if the doctor was interested in Alisha or whether he already knew her. Cameron returned to the Charger pondering several things. She needed to figure out why Jake was following this doctor and what it had to do with the event Daron was attending.

CHAPTER 18

Daron traced a finger over the black cotton material, amazed that the hat contained a layer of Kevlar. He had been surprised when Steve gave him a box from Cameron. Her notes said, *it may not save you from a high velocity round, but it should give you a fighting chance.* He parked the Maserati in the VIP area of the quaint south side reception hall then glanced over at Nicco Wolfe. Daron hoped things didn't get as crazy as the meeting with Calvin.

Damn. Has my life really come down to wearing bulletproof gear on a daily basis?

He definitely didn't like the fact that Levi was still searching for his place of residence. It meant Levi was closer to executing whatever he had planned. Daron hoped tonight would provide what he needed to shut Marquise down, then Levi would be next on the list.

Nicco lowered the window and launched three ghost drones before raising the glass.

They left the vehicle and moved swiftly to the door of the banquet hall.

"Mr. Wolfe and Mr. Kincaid, great seeing you," a bald security guard greeted them, holding the door open.

As their feet hit the black polished concrete floor in the reception room, Daron scanned the space which buzzed with conversation. The drones were set to record using a facial recognition program. If any of the people he had loaded passed by, the device would start recording. He handed the control tablet to two of the drones to Nicco.

"In and out in under thirty minutes." Daron said, wincing. He was still sore even though the doctor had given him a shot to help with the pain.

Nicco's blonde hair, blue eyes, and muscular physique immediately caught the attention of a gorgeous brunette, who motioned for him to join her. "Signal or text if you need me."

"Don't get too distracted." Daron nodded at the woman, whose shape was similar to Jennifer Lopez's. She leaned against one of the high boys with red under-lighting scattered around the outer edge.

Jazz music played softly in the background as Nicco and Daron made their way through the crowd, heading in separate directions.

Daron maneuvered through the attendees, occasionally stopping and talking with familiar faces until he reached a man with golden skin and platinum hair, who was his true target. He was supposed to have information on Marquise. Mitchell held up an index finger as he wrapped up a conversation.

Daron scanned the room and spotted Alisha and Ralph in a conversation with Zack Shaw, owner of several businesses, who was also known for contributing big dollars to community programs. Scott, The Castle security supervisor, who had been crossed off the suspect list, was at the bar standing too close to a woman that was not his wife. None of Marquise's top men were in the building, just a few minions.

Daron's head snapped toward the door. He couldn't believe his eyes.

Cameron walked in on the arm of a green-eyed Casanova, wearing an outfit Daron had bought for her, no less. The champagne halter dress hugged every curve like a second skin. Several male eyes were on her in an instant. She was expecting the attention because her eye color choice for tonight was emerald. It amazed him how small changes made Cameron look so different. Her face appeared thinner, her eyes seemed bigger, her full lips appeared smaller. He couldn't see the shoes but they were high enough to have her standing at 6'2".

Mitchell approached, forcing Daron's attention away from Cameron. "Sorry about that."

"I understand." Daron clasped the extended hand and shook it. Before he could utter any more words, Casanova and Cameron were by his side.

"Mitchell, wonderful event as usual." Casanova placed a hand on Mitchell's shoulder.

"Dr. Patrick Pine, your presence at my events makes them spectacular." Mitchell's eyes went from Cameron's face to her cleavage. "Who's this enchanting creature?"

"Jordan is *not* a creature," Dr. Pine frowned, pulling Cameron closer to his side before Daron could open his mouth to say anything.

Jordan. Daron glared at Cameron but she refused to make eye contact. Cameron was quick to set men straight. The fact that she simply gave Mitchell a mischievous but threatening smile then glanced up at Dr. Pine infuriated Daron. He thought about all the times she'd given him a hard time for doing something similar.

"She's an extremely intelligent and multi-talented *woman* who—"

"I didn't mean to offend," Mitchell held a palm up, then gestured to his left. "This is Daron Kincaid."

"Nice to meet you." Daron shook Dr. Pine's hand, then Cameron's, slowly caressing the back of hers with his thumb while looking deep into her eyes. "A pleasure seeing you."

Dr. Pine turned to Cameron. "Do you mind if I have a private conversation with Mitchell for a moment?"

"I don't mind at all."

Mitchell turned to Daron.

"It's fine," he answered before Mitchell said a word. He wanted a moment alone with *Jordan.*

Dr. Pine kissed Cameron on the cheek then excused himself as Mitchell escorted him down a back hallway.

"Jordan, huh?" Daron snatched a raspberry lemon drop martini from the passing butler's tray and handed the drink to Cameron. He placed a palm on her lower back, leading her to a highboy near the hallway where the two men had disappeared.

"He knows my name is Cameron." She swept the honey-brown hair over her shoulder. "It's also his brother's name."

Daron leaned into her ear. "Does he know your original eye color is hazel, that you have the most adorable set of dimples, and the most sensitive spot on your body is—"

"My green eye color was his request." Cameron stared at him as if she wasn't going to explain any further then polished off her drink before sitting the glass down on the table. "I'm going to grab a bite. I'll catch you later."

He gently captured her arm. "No, I got you. It's the least I could do after your gift saved my life." Daron quickly made his way to the buffet table. *Was Cameron really dating this Dr. Pine? Or was she up to something else?* Pulling up the drone feed of Dr. Pine and Mitchell talking on his cell, he entered the buffet line of people. Daron remembered how they met and couldn't discount Dr. Pine as a threat to getting Cameron back.

He glanced at Nicco, who was mingling in the center of the room but his eyes were on Daron. The people he recognized in the group were Zack and Tony Baltimore. Daron picked up a plate, made a selection of items she liked, returned to the table, and handed her a set of utensils and the full appetizer plate.

"Thanks." She unwrapped the utensils from the napkin.

Daron was curious because she wasn't using an alias, just her middle name. *How does she know him?* While he recognized her, he doubted those that didn't know her well would. "Have you figured out what's going on with your father?"

Cameron took a few bites of crab cake then said, "Not much to update. Jake seems to be narrowing down his Chicago list."

"Have you figured out the why?" Daron asked, glancing down at the cell to check the feed and saw Dr. Pine and Mitchell making their way down the hall and back toward the reception. His time with her was running out.

"Right now, I have Trenton combing through cold cases."

Daron hoped her being here with Dr. Pine was a means of obtaining information on her father and nothing more. "If you need help, let me know."

"I won't." Cameron moved the plate, playfully blocking his hand as he went for a crab cake. She glanced at him, eyes full of hunger he recognized wasn't for food. She shifted her attention across the room then turned to Daron. "We'll follow him a little while longer and see if we get more clues. Nicco's here with you tonight?"

"You wanted me to have a security detail," Daron fired back.

Something bigger was at play with Jake visiting all those doctors. He just didn't know what. The Castle was definitely in the middle of the situation but the bigger question was if the same person involved with Khalil's shooting was somehow connected to Jake's search for doctors.

"What brings you here tonight?" Cameron looked from Daron to Nicco then back to him just as her date returned.

"Daron, I must steal this beauty back from you and make up for the time I neglected her." Dr. Pine slid his arm possessively around Cameron's waist.

She placed a manicured hand in the center of Dr. Pine's chest. "You'll get away with nothing less."

The seductive tone of her statement was like someone scraping a key against the side panel of his Maserati. Daron had to remind himself to keep his feelings in check. *Focus.* Once he figured out who botched the security and dealt with Marquise, he and Cameron could work through the issues keeping them apart.

An older gentleman tapped Dr. Pine on the shoulder, causing him to look away.

Cameron snuggled deeper into Dr. Pine's side.

Daron moved toward Mitchell, whose eyes suddenly lit with fear. Cameron and her date disappeared into the crowd.

"Sorry, I've been so busy tonight but I see some other guests I need to greet." Mitchell's focus was across the room as he shook Daron's hand, sliding a flash drive into the palm.

"Another time."

Something was up. Daron sent a text to Nicco to keep an eye on Mitchell. He wasn't sure who spooked him but he now understood why this was the best environment to meet. With Mitchell hosting the event it wouldn't look strange for them to speak briefly.

Cameron and Dr. Pine slipped out of the door, which didn't put Daron in the best of moods.

Nicco made his way into the back corridor. Daron received a text from Pedro with an article with the picture of the stolen artwork from the auction Alisha had told him about.

Daron texted back. Don't tell me this is Reese and Amarion.

Pedro let him know they are lying low because they hadn't given the pieces to Marquise. Daron hated that they refused the offer to put them into a safe house but he couldn't force their help on the young men.

He sent a message to Steve to get a safe house prepared for them just in case, then went in search of Nicco. When Daron caught up with him, Mitchell was near a set of black steel doors being led down a long service hallway by two men in black suits. The two escorts held the silver handles then stepped closer to Mitchell as he exited the building.

A man with beady eyes and skin tone likened to a roasted coffee bean, a stocky Hispanic, and a burly White man jumped out, aiming their guns at Mitchell.

Daron signaled for Nicco to wait as he pulled up the drone feed and slid the listening device in one ear.

"Someone would like to speak to you."

"No shit, Sherlock. I couldn't tell by the two men escorting me out of my own event." Mitchell shook his head.

A Bentley Flying Spur drove up and Marquise stepped out. "Are you trying to get shot up like Khalil? If you're not, I suggest you keep Daron Kincaid off your guest list."

Daron ran a hand over the flash drive, knowing Mitchell definitely had the inside knowledge needed to bring Marquise down.

CHAPTER 19

The restaurant buzzed with the boisterous chatter of people enjoying a late lunch. Laughter and conversation filled the room but Daron was on a mission. Normally, he'd have Steve assign someone but he didn't want to put anyone else in Marquise's path. Plus, doing the job himself allowed him to take care of two tasks at once. One, confirm the identity of the person who helped Cedric in taking down The Castle's security and allowing Khalil to get shot. Two, attempt to take Marquise off the board long enough to help for Amarion and Reese. Daron settled at a table that gave him a view of the entrance but kept him obscure unless people walked directly past the table to see him. According to the information he received earlier, Marquise was currently meeting with a client in a private back room.

He texted Steve. Marquise is here. hopefully he incriminates himself.

Daron's cell pinged with a reply from Steve. He left out the back. The police have taken him into custody.

Right as Daron glanced at the time, a familiar face entered the restaurant heading to the reserved table. Terrell Ball slid his hand under the table to retrieve an envelope that was taped to the bottom. He scanned the area, seemingly trying to assess the privacy, then opened the envelope flipping quickly through the cash.

BAIT TAKEN was the next text sent to Daron.

The man was clueless about the setup. Steve would pick him up as he exited the restaurant, interrogate him and then call in the police.

Daron did a double-take as Roger entered the restaurant sporting a white suit. He marched past the hostess stand, heading into a semi-private room then pulled out a wicker chair from the table. A brunette woman lifted her hand, Roger brought it to his mouth and planted a kiss.

Daron glanced at his watch as the tall, leggy waitress approached.

"Can I get you anything else?" she smiled down at him.

"Just the bill." Daron smiled back, using the drone to record pictures of Roger and his dining partner.

The waitress slid the bill onto the table and Daron placed the cash on top.

"Keep the change."

"A pleasure serving you." She dropped her number on the table and sashayed away.

Ten minutes later, Roger stood and left the restaurant carrying a black briefcase.

Daron was right behind him.

Roger weaved his way through the crowd on Michigan Avenue, maneuvering to a less crowded street. He took long strides, stopping on the corner. Daron turned left, staying a few doors behind where a crowd of people were already gathered. A Bentley drove up, and an Asian man stepped out taking the briefcase from Roger and placing it in the trunk.

Daron moved a little closer to confirm the license plate before it drove off. He couldn't be concerned with that right now. The clock was ticking on getting the auction items back where they belonged and the young men out of town before Marquise was released.

CHAPTER 20

Daron watched the early morning news while putting the final touches on the plan to get Amarion and Reese straight. He'd already texted the young men the address of the safe house they were to meet him at in three hours. The faces of Reese and Amarion appeared on the screen listed as persons of interest in a recent art and jewelry heist.

What?

Neither of them had police records because they had never gotten caught. Now all of a sudden they were persons of interest. This had to be a maneuver to pressure them to deliver the items to Marquise. Daron fired off a text to Steve to see if Marquise had been released. Steve replied, Not yet but he has spoken with his lawyer. The cell rang, displaying Pedro's name.

"Do we know where they are?"

"Yes," Pedro replied, giving him an address on the west side of town then one on the south side.

"We have to get to them." Daron snatched the suit jacket, sliding it on. "We'll call the lawyers then take them down to the police station to work through this."

"I'll pick up Amarion," Pedro announced, keys clanging together in the background. "You find Reese."

Another familiar face appeared on the screen. "Hold on." Daron grabbed the remote and turned up the volume on the television.

The reporter announced in a solemn voice, "We have breaking news. Ralph Pullman has been arrested in connection with eight missing girls. The last place the girls were seen was at one of his enrichment programs. The community is in shock."

Daron pressed the mute button. "Shit."

"What?" Pedro asked, his engine turning over in the background.

"Ralph was arrested for trafficking," Daron rushed to his office, found a copy of the volunteer list and snapped a picture sending it to Steve with a note. "I need you to look over the file on him."

"You don't think he did it."

"No, but I do believe his program could have been utilized to select targets. The volunteers consist mainly of people who work in similar programs." Daron grabbed a few devices, sliding them into various pockets.

"I'll handle that after I pick up Amarion."

"Thanks." Daron's cell was ringing before he could place it in his pocket. He swiped to answer.

"Are you serious?" Steve asked with frustration in his voice.

"Absolutely. My top two candidates were in that room." Daron raced out to the Maserati. "I need to make sure they're not involved."

"Red's still in town. I'll see if he can look into it." Steve's farewell was barely heard before the click.

Daron rushed through side streets. He dialed Reese's number, but the call went to voicemail. Cedric's name popped up on the display.

"What's up?"

"They got Reese." Cedric's voice was barely above a whisper. "Dragged him out of his girlfriend's house and threw him in a van."

"You get back to the safehouse," Daron ordered then ended the call.

Daron's tracker alert for Amarion appeared on the screen but nothing for Reese. He pulled over to log into the system then linked the GPS app so that it would call whenever they changed directions.

"Currently on I-94 W," the automatic feminine voice with a slight British accent announced.

He headed to the expressway, noting they were ten minutes' worth of distance ahead of him. Depending on the traffic and the police presence on the expressway, he could catch up to them. Steve's name popped up on the screen seconds after the cell rang.

"A team has been dispersed. Mia is the lead."

"Tell them to stay a block out." Daron maneuvered in and out of cars, glad the traffic wasn't as heavy as expected and was steadily moving.

The instructions led him to a high rise north of downtown. The van pulled into the parking lot, and Daron drove past, turned onto the next block then put on his hazards. He launched the drone, guiding it around the corner and making it back to the van in time to see Reese walking with a black poster tube and silver box. Amarion was a few inches from him with hands tied behind his back being pushed toward the door by one of Marquise's goons.

Daron wasn't able to maneuver the drone to the elevator in time to slip in. *Damn.*

He dialed Mia.

"Hey, see if the team can access the thirty-second floor to get Amarion out safely." Daron pulled out his tablet. "I'm trying to find out what's housed there."

"We'll do the recon and let you know." Mia disconnected the line.

Daron flipped through, researching the building. A text came through from Reese. I MESSED UP. AT MARQUISE'S STRIP CLUB. PLEASE HELP. TYDL.

He stared at the *TYDL* for a while before he realized it was *tell you details later.*

A second text came through from Red this time. Midas wants to pass along some information to you tonight.

* * *

Daron left the Reese-Amarion situation in Mia's capable hands. By the time he made it home, changed, and headed back out, he'd been running late for the meeting. A ghost drone was launched as he made it along the brick wall to the chain-link fence near the alley. He attached a sensor on the wall so no one could sneak up behind him.

One of Marquise's enforcers, along with Midas and Bobby, the red-haired man from the shooting the night of Ralph's event, were arguing at the end of the block.

Daron was too far off to hear their conversation and the drone wasn't within range to pick up sound. Had he known it was Midas who had gotten shot that night, Daron would have made it a point to visit him in the hospital.

A gunshot rang out.

Daron stepped behind the cover of the wall as the two remaining men scanned the area for potential witnesses. The goon bent over and felt Midas' neck for a pulse, then looked at the Bentley, and shook his head. This wasn't exactly what Daron expected to record when he came. The warning sensor went off, Daron turned to see Cameron quietly approaching.

What in the hell is she doing here?

"We need to go," she whispered, hooking her arm under his and guiding him toward the Legacy he'd driven.

Daron retrieved the drone, trying to keep up with her pace. "Meet me at my house and don't make me come find you."

He was fuming as he drove home. *If she doesn't show up ...*

Trailing him was unacceptable. Daron was equally upset that he hadn't noticed her before she'd been a few feet away. Cameron drove into the driveway minutes after he'd parked the Legacy.

"I don't believe you," Daron growled as she stepped out of the Charger. "You're following me. Why?"

Cameron walked up and leaned beside the door, waiting to enter. "What were you doing there?"

"I'll respond after you answer me." Daron unlocked the door and followed her into the house.

She crossed her arms, giving him a steely stare. "Why do you think?"

"Just answer the damn question." He stalked to the refrigerator and yanked out a Heineken.

"You're the one with the questionable actions." She snatched the bottle out of Daron's hand and sat it on the counter behind her.

He reached around her and reclaimed his beer. "What is it that you think I was doing?

"Recruiting." Cameron's eyes narrowed on him. "Which I assume is a contributing factor to me being attacked every time I turned around."

"I'd never dishonor my mother's memory like that." Daron was disgusted because he thought Cameron knew him well enough to know that.

"Interesting you mentioned dishonoring your mom's memory and not your dad's."

Was she making that statement because his father and Bishop were best friends? Words have power. Use them wisely.

Daron closed his eyes briefly as he inhaled and exhaled before speaking. "What's your issue?"

"I've been threatened more as a regular citizen than I've ever been working for Bishop." She tugged at the black t-shirt he was wearing. "You're the one having clandestine meetings where people get shot. Hell, *you* got shot. You can't fault me for wondering if you had reverted to old ways."

He downed the amber liquid, then took another breath, trying to reign in the anger before he allowed words to tumble out of his mouth that he couldn't retract. "Maybe you need my program just as much as these young men."

She flinched. "What do you mean by that?" She followed him around the kitchen island as he headed into the entertainment room.

Daron spun around to face her. "I'm going to ask you a couple of the questions I asked your cousin." He lifted two fingers then pointed his index finger at her. "What part of your past are you enslaved to? What small things have you done to free yourself?"

"I'm not enslaved to the past," she snapped.

"So, you've talked to your father about the day he left you and JD in jail and took your brothers and their friends' home?" Daron lowered himself onto the couch, picking up the remote.

"No, I've moved beyond that."

"You haven't. Otherwise, you would've learned how to come to me and talk about things instead of cutting me off, avoiding me, and drawing your own conclusions." He turned on the television. "You can go."

Cameron snatched the remote, muting the sound, before dropping it on the ottoman directly in front of him as she sat. "My situation with Jake is not the same."

"Oh, but it is." He leaned forward in her face, staring into those dark-brown eyes that held so much disbelief. "You've never spoken to your father about what happened. You avoid him every time someone attempts to put the two of you in the same room."

She frowned, the action marring her beautiful features. "What difference will it make?"

"You won't know because you won't try." He picked up the remote again, leaned back on the couch and unmuted the television. "Just like my situation isn't all it appears to be."

Cameron huffed. "Maybe I'll try once I stop being attacked on the streets on a regular basis."

"Misdirection, eh? I need my queen to be able to communicate with me." Daron shifted his position in order to see the flat screen. "I would have explained everything to you."

"Stop lying." Cameron bounced to her feet. "I'm not your queen because you issued an ultimatum, as if I was the one in the bar putting a man in a headlock and throwing out threats like I was no longer retired."

Daron received an icy glare. *Damn.* That statement double-tapped him in the heart, forcing him to accept the truth. He had not been forthcoming since he found out about The Castle. While he'd give her that, she was going to have to take responsibility for her contribution to their problems. "I'm not sure you'll ever be able to have a healthy relationship with anyone until you stop running from whatever it is that scares you."

"Don't make this about me and my father." She crossed both arms, issuing an evil glare. "I came to check on you and talk. Maybe see if you were up for a late dinner. When I arrived, you were trotting out in a black jogging suit tipping down the street. You weren't going for a jog or going to the Jaguar, Porsche, or the Maserati, you climbed into a Subaru Legacy, the stealth car."

"Are you *sure* it's not about you?" Daron shifted his entire body toward her. "Your armor of choice is avoiding your dad and hiding behind your training facility. And redirecting conversation to everything but the real issue."

"Don't turn things on me." Cameron headed toward the door, then stopped, glaring at him as if she was sick to her stomach. "Because of you, I almost feel the need to wear my Kevlar suit every day."

"How is helping people get in shape and occasionally teaching self-defense class supposed to help good people not get caught in the life you left?" Daron challenged, leaping to his feet and trailing her through the hall.

She paused near the kitchen island. "It doesn't look like it's going too well for you."

"It's going just fine. These are just growing pains of building something that has an impact and people who don't want to see it happen." Daron reached for her arm, preventing her from walking away. "Funny enough this wasn't my original plan, until I met a woman named Tandria, who claimed she was going to use her skills to help people."

"Oh no, you don't get to do that." Cameron huffed, snatching her arm away. "I have a plan and it requires me getting my gym facility up and running. Not going off half-assed to prove a point to any damn body."

"I'm saying you inspire me to continue making a difference in people's lives." Daron glanced at the colorful canvas on the dining room wall. "Every day I see JD's painting hanging on the wall it motivates me to keep going."

"JD's purpose doesn't require him to risk his life and freedom as well as those who work for him. Mine does," she fired back, stalked toward the door then turned toward him. "You're trying to make it about me when this is really about the fact that you were less than honest and it made me question your actions." Cameron threw up her hands and went to the door.

Daron activated the security so she couldn't leave. "You want me to be honest with you then you have to be open to hearing the truth."

She released the knob and spun around glaring at him. "I am."

"If I told you what's going on, could you have listened without immediately passing judgment?"

"I'm not one to take people at their word with certain things, especially when their actions don't match said words." The accusatory tone of Cameron's voice grated on his nerves. "I'm going to verify until we reach a certain level of trust. Remember, our former lives have taught us to be excellent hiders of the truth."

Daron couldn't argue that point with her. "I don't live in the past."

She pulled on the knob. "Open the damn door."

She was right. Their relationship was too new and hadn't reached that level of trust yet. Especially considering how they met. "Yes, the things that happened have made me more cautious, but I had to learn the hard way that dwelling in the past will cost you too much of your present and future happiness."

"Full disclosure." She leaned on the door with a hand still resting on the doorknob. "In order for me to stay retired, I can't be with a man who's about that life. And I expressed that to you."

Cameron had voiced her concerns at the beginning of the Katara-Tracy situation and The Castle business only brought those issues to the forefront again.

"But you still hang with your friends who are in and have no desire to come out," Daron countered.

"Yes, but they have a network to rely on. I would be their hail mary. And let's just call a spade a spade." She reached into the pocket of her jacket. retrieving her car keys. "It's not the same emotions at play with them."

"Look I'm not trying to bring Kimura out of retirement, which is why I'm trying to make my program public and have someone else help

Pedro run it."

"Not Alisha."

"Maybe Alisha." Daron wasn't going to argue with her about his candidate choice. Especially since he was trying to reserve judgment until he knew what exactly was going on with Alisha. "We are still in the process of selecting candidates to approach."

Daron's alarm sounded, and he pulled the tablet out to see three men approaching the house.

Cameron rushed to look at the screen. "What's going on?'

"Someone's attempting to break in."

Cameron reached under her jacket and pulled out a Ruger.

"Not this place." Daron retrieved his cell from the jogging pants' pocket and called the police. He kept his focus on three men, who ran from the house as he disconnected the line. "They couldn't have searched the house in that short amount of time."

"Is that why you aren't driving the Jag?"

"Yeah, I parked over at that property. Now the Porsche and Maserati are here since they're registered to one of my corporations." Daron slid on his jacket and left the house with Cameron on his tail.

The police had arrived by the time they drove up. Seconds later, an explosion and flames erupted from the house.

Daron immediately suspected the officers were on someone's payroll. They were rarely that quick, despite being several yards up the street.

"Did they really just blow up my house?" Daron stared out of the window at the grey smoke cloud billowing into the air. He pulled out the tablet, accessing the drone across the street. Then he rewound the video feed to see how the men had entered the property.

After they couldn't get in through the door or break the window, they dropped the incendiary device in the chimney. One of the men barely made the jump to the roof next door and out of range before the house exploded.

"They're done warning you."

CHAPTER 21

Cameron's cell rang. She checked the display. Daron. She felt bad for not answering but he almost had her convinced that he wasn't involved in criminal activities and then his house was blown up. If Jake was actually sick, she didn't need to get involved with anything that terminated her own retirement. So far, Trenton hadn't found a connection to anything in the media. Jake could just be paranoid.

As law enforcement, her father had put people away from all walks of life. Her mother may not have been so off the mark to be concerned about Jake. The entire situation was frustrating. She had been enjoying a semi-normal life now. Cameron missed Daron being a part of her daily routine but whatever he had going on was dangerous. These men were a little too determined to use her as leverage against him. They clearly didn't get the memo that they were no longer together. Or they had and didn't believe it.

Cameron watched as the man approached the community center carrying light-pink roses with a dark fuchsia trim. Beautiful, but they immediately put her on the defense. Daron was aware of the main reason she didn't like bouquets.

The delivery guy grinned. "It seems that someone wanted you to know you're special."

"You can keep them and give them to your girlfriend." Cameron continued moving swiftly toward her car. Bishop had her leery of accepting them, even when they were sent from someone she knew, as well as sniffing perfume in department stores. He told her that as skilled as she was, she couldn't kick ass if she was drugged.

"They smell wonderful." He held them toward her face.

She knocked them away.

He tried again.

Something was definitely wrong. She snatched them out his hand and pressed them into his face. "Describe the scent."

He jerked his head to the right. Cameron punched him in his gut and stuffed the roses in his face. His body collapsed. The floral van doors whipped open and two large men rushed out. "We wanted to do this the easy way."

"By drugging me? Interesting." Cameron unclipped the gun holster. "I'm down for the hard way."

She fired at the door, forcing the men to jump back and close it as she ran toward her vehicle for cover. Out the corner of her eye, a lanky man approached and fired a taser. She turned her body. The barbed darts missed connecting with her flesh by millimeters.

One of the men from the van scrambled across the street and rushed her. Cameron blocked his jab, but the needle pricked her skin. She immediately released the guy, grabbing the grey bead off her bracelet before sinking the needle in her thigh. The drug would slow down the effect of whatever she'd been given but she needed to get to safety. She jammed an elbow into the guy behind her, pulled the needle out of her neck and slammed one of her black beads to his chest, then flung him into the other man. Cameron pressed her earring as she raced to the Charger. She slid behind the wheel, locking the door and gasping for breath.

Her hand slammed down on the red button on her dashboard to engage protection mode. A smoked glass rose to cover the windows. The man who reached for the door handle screamed as the blades dropped, slicing into his hand. Another man banged with a gun trying to break the glass.

Pulling out her phone, she tried to dial Greg but her eyes felt like lead. The banging quieted as the phone slipped from her fingers and she faded into darkness.

* * *

A beeping noise like a truck backing up filtered into Cameron's mind. Loud voices seemed to be in a heated debate. The men who attacked her were attempting to tow her car. They would have a difficult time hooking it up with the protection system engaged. The Charger dropped a shield from the undercarriage to the ground so they couldn't easily access what they needed to take the car away. She could hear Daron's voice as she struggled to open her eyes.

"Greg. How in the hell do I get into the car?"

The sound of flesh connecting with glass echoed in the air. Cameron tried to turn her head with no success. Her mouth was so dry. Eyes heavy like lead. Her body felt like it was pinned to the seat.

"I saw the blades on the handle," Daron roared. "She's not moving. I need to open the damn door."

Seven taps on the glass, then the locks clicked. "I'm in. I got her."

"Cam, baby talk to me." Daron's fingers slid to her neck, searching for a pulse.

"What in the hell have you gotten yourself into?" Cameron managed to say as she came out of her fog. Her body was still not quite cooperating but her mind and mouth were in gear.

He slowly shifted her body toward his, resting his forehead on hers.

"Is she all right?" Pedro asked, peering in over Daron's shoulder.

"Not quite. Drive my car to the house." Daron stood, passing Pedro his keys.

Pedro's eyes went large as dinner plates and his mouth hung open for a moment before a smile crept over his face.

Daron lifted her from behind the steering wheel. "I'm driving her to

Little Company of Mary to get her checked out."

Pedro practically skipped over to a dark-grey Maserati Quattroporte. Now she understood Pedro's earlier expression.

"I don't need to get checked out. Take me to my house," Cameron insisted as Daron escorted her around to the passenger side. "I need to sleep it off."

"Do it for me?" Daron closed the door and returned to the driver's side.

"I'm serious. Don't take me to the hospital," she warned. The hospital made her an easy target. Too many strangers and not enough weapons to protect herself. It would be difficult to know for sure who was staff and who was there to harm her.

"Fine, but you *will* be checked out." Daron sent a text before pulling off. "Tell me what happened. By the time I got here, they had a tow truck backed up to the car."

Cameron's eyes still felt heavy and her mind still had its sluggish moments as she told him what transpired. She noticed that he ignored the instructions to take her home and was aiming for his house instead.

"How are you feeling?" Daron brushed back the loose strands of hair from her forehead as they sat at a red light. "You're sure you don't want to go to the hospital."

"Positive." Cameron reached for the bottle of water in the gym bag on the floor near her feet. "Let's talk about your situation."

"My situation." Daron turned as the vehicle in front of him proceeded through the green light. He did a quick check in the rearview mirror.

"These men are determined to have leverage on you." Cameron paused as a wave of nausea hit her. She sipped the water then asked, "Why is that?"

"Bishop left me a membership for a place called The Castle." Daron glanced at her as he parked beside the Quattroporte as though trying to gauge her reaction.

"Why didn't you tell me?" Cameron closed her eyes for a moment, resting the back of her head against the seat. *More Secrets.*

"I wanted to know exactly what it was and who was part of it before bringing up the subject with you." He lowered the window to retrieve the keys from Pedro.

"Take care of her," Pedro ordered.

"I will," Daron replied as Pedro made his way to a white BMW.

Cameron studied Daron's profile as he raised the window. "I feel like that statement you made prior to Pedro's arrival was a partial truth but I'm going to let it slide." She stared at the sleek maroon vehicle the Maserati was parked behind. "You bought another car."

"Testing it out for a friend." Daron left the driver's seat with the swiftness of a child being chased by a dog. She knew he'd just issued yet another half-true statement.

Daron rounded the Charger, helping her out. She hadn't expected Daron to lift and carry her.

He winced a bit. Daron gave her that stern non-negotiable glare, which meant he must have felt her resistance. No denying that she was falling in love with the man. Had it been anyone else, she would have made them put her down.

The fact that "retirement" didn't mean the same to him as it did to her, and the fact that his life had put her in a situation where he needed to carry her, reinforced her decision. At the rate that these people were hunting her down, she was fine standing by his side if he was caught up in something out of his control. But if he was actively back in the business, she couldn't deal with that. Right now, if anything happened to him or someone close to them, she'd hunt the bastards down and make them regret it.

CHAPTER 22

After the doctor came by to check Cameron out, Daron set up a workstation in the bedroom to keep an eye on her.

His cell vibrated on the portable desk, just as Cameron's chimed on the nightstand. He glanced at his screen to see Steve's name. He snatched his phone from the black metal surface and headed to the hallway.

"What's up?" He kept his tone low enough not to wake her even though she seemed to sleep through her phone ringing.

"Amarion has been relocated several times since yesterday," Steve explained.

"I hate the team just missed extracting them." Daron was frustrated. By the time the team made it past Marquise's guards, the boys were being taken out the back via a secret freight elevator.

"I noticed Reese's tracker had been activated." Steve's voice seemed hesitant as if he was questioning Daron's decision. Cameron's phone rang again.

"Clearly he did not mention the tracker to Marquise's men." Daron leaned on the door frame watching the rise and fall of her chest.

"Whatever you say," Steve muttered and the displeasure in his tone became obvious. "I'll send you a summary of what Terrell said."

"Good." He received the rest of the update and let Steve know how Cameron was doing before ending the call.

Daron turned his attention to the package from JD which had arrived earlier in the day. It reminded him that he needed to talk to Cameron's old team about taking a job to handle switching out some artwork for him.

The art pieces Reese and Amarion took hadn't left the building with them. While he could take down the security system, even with Calvin's suit, he knew breaking, entering and recovery wasn't his area of expertise. It was one thing to send his security teams in to rescue someone but he couldn't send them in to deal with stolen auction pieces. Something kept nagging him about the conversation he'd had with Cedric.

I need to reassess the list of The Castle suspects.

There had to be a second person working with the security system on the day of Khalil's shooting. Reviewing the conversation Steve had with Terrell before turning him over to law enforcement moved to the top of his to-do list. Then he would work on his plan to replace the stolen items with fakes, then leverage the real ones to get Reese and Amarion back.

Cameron's phone chimed again, as it had been doing often for the last two hours. Most of the text and missed calls were from one person she had listed as *Dr. Feelgood*. Daron didn't even want to think about her seeing someone else, let alone being intimate with another man.

The phone rang and Aretha Franklin's voice filled the room. Cameron groaned and rolled over, tangling the beige sheets around her body, then disconnected the charger and answered the call.

"I'm so sorry," she said in a soft and sensual tone, then paused listening as her head returned to the pillow. "I'm fine. I had a small crisis at work and completely forgot about our date tonight."

Daron stared at her, straining to hear the other side of the conversation but could only catch a few words here and there.

"Yes, I'll see you then." Cameron extended her arm, returning the phone to the nightstand. She laid there a few moments with her eyes closed before peeling back the sheet and taking careful steps to make it to the restroom.

Although he knew she wasn't trying to get to him since she didn't know she'd be there, the jealousy monster still reared its ugly head. Daron hadn't expected her to start dating so soon. His eyes were glued to the nightstand with Aretha's voice haunting him. Like a teenager, he was tempted to call to see what ringtone she had for him.

"What has you frowning like that?"

His head snapped toward Cameron who was moving back toward the bed. Daron would be damned if he'd tell her what was really bothering him. He glanced at the laptop's screen. "When I say that I hate asking you this, I mean it from the bottom of my heart. Do you think you could contact your old team to see if they could switch the real stolen auction pieces for fakes?"

"Why?"

"It may be the only way to save Amarion and Reese." Daron was grateful her cousin was able to get a copy done so fast. It seems Bishop had equipment that made duplicates that could get past an untrained eye easily.

"I'm sure they'll do it if I ask. Give me the details." Cameron retrieved the cell, then lowered herself onto the bed.

"I confirmed where they're holding the items. While I can get through their security system—" Daron hated not having more time to put this plan together. "—grabbing the pieces without damaging them isn't my forte."

"How many items and how many guards?" Cameron asked.

"It's two items; a necklace and a painting. Three guards." Daron was having second thoughts. If anything happened to Cameron's team, she would never forgive him. However, he needed local people he could trust to be discreet.

"I'll see if Kathleen is still in town and the two of us will handle it."

Daron closed the laptop. "I need your contacts to do it, not you."

"Why make my team a target when The Castle member in question has already seen the two of us." Cameron gathered up the phone charger. "We can get in and out undetected if your intel is right."

"What if I'm wrong? No."

She stepped in front of his makeshift desk, leaning in toward him. "You trust my old team to handle the job, but you don't trust me?"

"Cam, I can't ask you to do that. I won't have you do it." Daron knew she'd be resistant to the next idea he was about to present. "However, I do want you to reconsider training the women from the shelter on weapons."

"That's more dangerous to me than doing this favor for you." Cameron slipped out of his grasp and snatched her jacket from the chaise. "I know and trust Kathleen. These other women could get innocent men and women killed if they don't know how to keep their mouths shut."

He stood in front of her, staring deeply into those brown orbs that expressed a world of doubt. "These innocent women could die if you don't teach them how to protect themselves. If what occurred today with you, happens to them … the majority of them would not have survived."

Cameron was silent for a moment, her brows furrowed and her lips taut. "Here's the deal." She placed an index finger in the center of his chest. "*You* will purchase each one a black tier specialty membership and refer them to Tandria. Once you have the memberships, I'll show you a separate entrance into the facility to access the gun range and other weaponry training areas to show the ladies how to get in. They're not to use the regular entrance to the gym facility."

"Wait, you have a weapons training area?"

"Just because I haven't actively been helping people and have been a little leery about implementing my plan, doesn't mean I'm not working toward the goal." She moved around him heading out of the bedroom.

"When were you going to tell me?" Daron asked as Cameron went into the refrigerator, pushed the Heineken aside and grabbed a bottle of water.

"I did." She twisted off the cap, downed the entire contents then tossed the bottle. "Clearly you didn't believe me."

Daron inhaled, trying to remember that conversation. "Put me on your schedule to tour the place about five tomorrow evening."

"My schedule is full for the remainder of the week." She smiled sweetly, letting him know she was intentionally being difficult.

"How were you going to help me out with the other situation?" Daron hated being on the receiving end of her stubborn, ornery ways.

"I'd willingly change my plans to help you out, but not for you to do a tour."

He moved closer to her. "I'll be there tomorrow and you *will* show me."

All the pretend lightheartedness left her expression as she glared at him, pursed her lips, then looked him up and down. "Fine."

Daron recognized that 'I plan to be difficult' tone and knew he'd have to double down to make sure she didn't avoid him.

"I'm going to get out of your way." She headed for her gym shoes near the door.

Daron leaned on the wall, his eyes glued to her shapely ass as she bent over to put on a pair of black Nikes. "You know I always enjoy spending time with you. How about you let me feed you while we discuss the possibility of Greg and Rob doing that job?"

She glanced up. Her lips slowly curving into a smile as she slipped off the shoes that she'd stepped into. Daron was glad he was good in the kitchen because Cameron's love language was food. If he could get her to sit down to eat, he had a shot. The moment he couldn't, he was met with that unbending, unwavering, and stubborn woman her father had been battling to get back into her life.

She followed him into the kitchen. "Their business model changed when I left," Cameron explained, referring to Greg and Rob, two men who handled reclaiming stolen items and returning them to their owners for a hefty fee.

Daron opened the stainless-steel door and scanned his choices as she settled in at the kitchen island. "You're saying you don't think they can handle it."

"I'm saying they don't take last minute requests. I'm not sending them in without proper time to plan. There's barely enough time to do what's necessary to successfully get in and out."

"But I'm supposed to be comfortable sending *you* and Kathleen in." He pulled out shrimp, deciding to make a scampi and garlic bread. Her favorites.

"To be honest, I could handle this by myself *with* the proper planning." She picked up the remote, turning on the jazz station on the stereo in the dining room. "This will require split-second decisions and it helps to have a partner to assist with any unexpected glitches."

He mulled it over for a while. "You know what?" Daron chopped the garlic, parsley, and tomatoes as the pasta cooked. "I'll just donate double the last posted bid before it was stolen."

"You're going to donate two million dollars and not expect to come under scrutiny especially with your new association with The Castle." Cameron swiped a banana off the tiered display and peeled the fruit.

"The money is clean and I don't mean it has been laundered." Daron tried not to get distracted as Cameron's lips slid over the length of the banana before she took a bite. His body immediately reacted to the sensual devouring of the fruit. The things that woman could do with her tongue. He missed those lips on him. Those thick thighs wrapped around his waist. Those breasts pressed against his chest. Her cell chimed and even though the song wasn't playing, Aretha's voice entered his thoughts, frustrating him even more. "Clean, as in I earned it legally."

"That's all well and good. But do you really want to step in the spotlight again?" Cameron swiped a thumb across the screen of the cell, typed something, then turned it face down on the countertop.

She was right about who should handle things but Daron didn't want to be the one to take her out of retirement, not even for a night. "I can handle it."

"You just got on me about not using my skills to *help people out*. Now you present an opportunity for me to do that and you're backtracking." She reached for a slice of bread and popped it into her mouth.

Daron tapped the back her hand. "Cut it out. You won't want any of the good stuff if your stomach's full."

"Oh, I always want some of your good stuff," she said, and they both laughed.

He drained the pasta, added the shrimp to the sauce to cook while the bread warmed on the grill. "Fine, but if you do it, include me in the plans," Daron said, getting the conversation back on topic.

"What?"

Daron couldn't see her facial expression but could feel her eyes drilling into his back. "I can take down the security system, keep watch for trouble, and drive the getaway car."

"This isn't what you do," she voiced in a soft tone as if being careful not to insult him.

"Security systems are my thing and I'm fully capable of being behind the wheel." He tilted the pan so the pasta slid into one of the two bowls.

"You?" She tightened her lips as if she was choosing her words carefully.

"I can't ask you to take a risk that I'm not willing to take." He slid a bowl toward her. "If you're in, *I'm* in."

"Fine." She slid off the stool and grabbed the Pinot Grigio, then poured two glasses of their typical pairing for the dish he prepared.

"Cam, you know we're good together," Daron asserted, accepting a glass and letting his finger stay on hers. "Let's try to work on getting back on the right track."

"I don't know." Cameron palmed the car keys on the counter. "I have to admit it hurt more than I thought it would that you chose The Castle over us."

"I distinctly remember you tossing my keys back at me and walking away … from us."

Cameron turned her lips up at him, twirled her keys around a finger, then stopped their movement by catching them in her fist. Her gaze was filled with sadness as she stared at him. "I don't know if you can be my King *and* a King of The Castle."

"You're being unreasonable." Daron huffed.

"You're the one who gave me an ultimatum because I asked you questions about the bar incident. I know what kind of relationship I want." Cameron took a sip of wine and stood. "While I don't expect to know every detail, considering what your company does, I do expect to know when you're about to make a decision that could change our lives."

"It's not what you did, it's *how* you did it," he shot back.

"Let's talk about swapping out these pieces of art." Cameron's gaze searched his face as if she was trying to determine if she was walking away or staying.

"No." Daron blocking her exit from the stool. "Maybe if we were in a committed relationship, I would have told you about The Castle."

Cameron crossed her arms. "Maybe if you would have, we'd be in one."

"I also know what I want in a relationship and that is a woman who doesn't walk away without hesitation at the first sign of trouble."

"Maybe I wouldn't have if we hadn't already had a conversation, before pursuing a relationship, about honesty. Neither one of us were supposed to be living a life that required us to keep stuff from each other, outside of specified details that violated our client privacy."

"The Castle is my client."

"The membership from Bishop was not." Cameron gently pushed him in the center of his chest, causing him to grimace. "Either we discuss where you think the items are being held or I'm heading home."

Daron remained in her path, debating whether to let go of the conversation on the state of their relationship. "Have a seat, but know this conversation isn't over. It's just on pause."

She stared him down a few seconds before reclaiming her spot.

This incident should have brought them closer together, but instead, he realized how close he was to permanently losing her. He felt a sudden rush of emotion thinking about the fact that at least she was there to argue with him. Had today turned out differently, she could have been held captive by Marquise, or dead. "Are you absolutely sure your old team can't handle this?"

"Are you being sexist?" She frowned, before taking a bite of the scampi.

"No."

Cameron snarled, "Then tell me the location."

Daron prepared himself for the *what the hell* look as he said, "The storage room in a private strip club."

CHAPTER 23

Daron and Steve spent over an hour discussing how to handle the situation with Marquise and the young men. The risks were too great to set up a trade. If Marquise double-crossed him, Daron could end up trying to explain why he was in possession of the stolen items. The final decision was to lure Marquise away from the house with a business offer while the team infiltrated the mansion and retrieved Amarion and Reese.

"Why didn't you tell me Cameron was attacked after her self-defense class before they attempted to drug her." Steve closed up his laptop.

His head snapped toward Steve. "Because she didn't mention it." Daron hated getting information about her second hand.

"Dude, she shot off a man's middle finger," Steve stated, packing up his bag. "Said she was being nice, she wanted to put a bullet in his temple."

"Cameron is a badass on any given day of the week but these fools are going to mess around and unleash Bishop's Kimura." Daron glanced at Cameron's picture on his desk as he grabbed the jacket off the chair.

Steve raised a bushy eyebrow. "And she's going to start leaving a body count."

"Dammit, she should have agreed to a security detail." Daron slipped on his jacket, scanning the area to make sure he had everything he needed. "I can't allow this situation to continue touching her like this."

"Look, fortunately she has the skills that makes it hard to be taken down easily but those same skills make it difficult to discreetly watch her back." Steve slid the bag strap onto his shoulder.

"Don't I know it," Daron said, pulling out his keys. The security team assigned to Cameron couldn't track her even with the use of the ghost drone. She had swiped a set of prototype contacts, which gave her the ability to see the clear drone. This was a small taste of what Jake had to deal with over the years and Daron didn't like it one bit. "Cam has managed to shake every attempt to watch over her. How do you know about the incident?"

"Found out when I gave Red a tour of Cam's gym facility, since she couldn't be found at the time." Steve's face went taut. "Did you know Lex was in the city?"

"Recently?" Daron asked, trailing Steve to the back door.

"This morning." Steve waited as Daron locked up. "As I was walking Red to his car, we saw her and Lex together in the covered garage."

"Lex knew and didn't tell us?" Daron tried his best not to jump to any conclusions by creating his own scenarios of why she and Lex were meeting.

"I don't know. He was gone by the time we reached her. He's flying to a conference, so I can't reach him." Steve glanced at his Rolex. "For another hour or so."

"How did you find out then?" Daron paused at the door of the Lamborghini Urus.

"Red was teasing her about it, but he thought we already knew."

"I need you to change strategy. Someone needs to shadow her and at least make sure she isn't followed when she leaves her class," Daron said as he slid behind the wheel.

During the entire twenty-five-minute drive to meet Cameron, Daron tried not to think about Lex being with Cameron without telling anyone. He valet parked at the hotel connected to Weber Grill and took his ticket, then headed in. The smoky grill smell greeted him as he made his way past the bar to Cameron. She stood near the hostess desk, dressed in black distressed jeans, and a simple v-neck shirt. She was typing into her cell.

"Hello, gorgeous." He gave her a hug when she looked up.

The waitress led them to a booth.

"I heard you saw Lex and Red," Daron said, attempting to keep his tone casual.

"Yes." She smiled sweetly then asked, "Is Alisha's home nice? I heard you had the opportunity to check it out."

"Yes, I escorted her home because of a shooting that took place after Ralph's event, but nothing happened." Daron decided to leave the subject of Lex alone and wait until they ordered to come clean about why he asked her to meet him there. He needed to take time to lay the groundwork for reconciliation by reminding her how they were together before Tracy went missing and that inherited membership to the Castle. Dinner was supposed to be about rekindling their love, not getting into the argument.

"This is not a prime spot to discuss business." She eyed him suspiciously, especially since he requested that she come alone.

Daron ordered their usual starter sampler, chopped chicken salad, smoked beef brisket, and filet mignon. "I no longer need you and Kathleen to switch out items."

"What?"

"Yes, I could have told you over the phone," he said, when her expression darkened, "But I'll use any excuse to spend some time with you."

"Good strategy coming clean *after* you ordered our food." Cameron chuckled, moving the cell to make room for the waitress to sit the appetizer sampler.

It felt like old times as they talked and dined until his cell rang with a call from the one person he couldn't ignore. He answered, "Steve, what's up?"

Daron listened as Steve explained that Brandi was involved in an incident.

"Everything all right?" Cameron asked as he disconnected and motioned to the waitress.

"My aunt is in trouble. She was taken into a house at gunpoint."

* * *

Roger Hare's hustle paid him well, according to the Stowe modular sofa from Bentley, in his living room, the Galileo table from Fendi in the dining room, and the Gianoberto lamps from Bugatti throughout the house. Daron moved further into the living room as Steve searched the house for Brandi. Cameron remained near the door keeping watch. The older man stepped out of the back hall, wearing a pair of designer blue jeans and a t-shirt.

A younger man opened the front door and entered the living room. "Boss. You good?"

"He's currently occupied. You'll have to come back," Cameron ordered, stepping in front of him.

He moved forward. "Nah, it don't work like that."

Roger ordered, "Handle her."

Daron chuckled, looking back at the boy who had a wide stance to accommodate his sagging pants. "If he wants to get his ass served to him, he can try."

Cameron extended her gold wand and released the blades.

"I'll be back, Sweetie." The young man backed out the door. "We'll see how well you two handle what's coming."

"Stop playing games and tell me where Brandi is." Daron was curious about what his aunt had on this man.

"I understand people being scared of your brother, but you? Nah." Roger stalked across the space.

"Remember, I was raised with Troy." Daron slid his cell into his pocket. "Don't let my appearance fool you. I'm not the one."

"Oh, is that right?" Roger's fist came flying toward Daron's face.

He dodged and countered with a jab to Roger's jaw. When Roger returned the punch, Daron slipped an arm under Roger's, grabbed his shoulder, and slammed him down on the Galileo table. Pulling the Beretta from his waistband, Daron pressed the barrel against the man's forehead. "When I said I'm not the one, I meant that shit."

He glanced at Cameron who wore a sexy grin and a lust-filled glare. She gave him a wink. The air crackled with a sexual charge that sent currents of desire careening through his system. Daron had to tear his eyes away from her and refocus on the situation. "Where is my aunt?"

"I'm sorry man," Roger squawked. "I asked my men to detain her until I got home." Roger held the free hand up as if he was contemplating whether he could grab the gun and not get shot. "Bee should've minded her business. I didn't mean—"

"Where. Is. She?" Daron pressed the muzzle harder into the man's forehead.

"I had nothing to do with your brother's death." Roger glanced at the front door as if he was expecting backup. "I couldn't let her come around to my spots causing trouble."

"What did you do to her?"

"You might need to speed up the interrogation," Cameron announced.

Daron glanced back to see Cameron looking out the door and reaching for her gun. Not a good sign. Steve rushed the living room and shook his head.

Daron moved the barrel to Roger's mouth. "Are you going to make me ask you again?"

"She probably went to the cemetery to visit her brother."

Cameron touched Steve's shoulder. "We need to handle this."

Daron couldn't see what was drawing her attention but Steve lifted his gun and, flanking Cameron, moved toward the door. He snatched Roger by the collar of his shirt and lifted him to his feet. "If she's hurt, know that when I'm done with you, you'll wish I'd killed you."

Steve and Cameron raced out the door with Daron seconds behind. Three men approached the house and four more moved rapidly up the street. Cameron stood with a gun in each hand, her gaze flickering from house to street.

"Cam, go get my aunt just in case Roger sends someone after her," Daron commanded. As capable as she was, his instinct was to protect her.

"I'll text you when I have her." Cameron slid her guns into the holsters and pulled out that gold wand.

Steve shifted until his back was positioned to allow him to watch the house and the street. "Let's try to send these boys to the hospital, not the morgue."

"Shit," Daron muttered as Steve barely finished the sentence before he realized that Cameron had run a direct route to her car, right through the three men that now writhed in pain on the ground near the curb.

Roger stepped out on the porch and whistled. His men halted their approach. "I'll stay away from Brandi, *if* she stays away from me." He returned to the house.

Daron and Steve cautiously moved to their vehicles, then headed to the cemetery to catch up with Cameron and Brandi. He hadn't even thought about the fact that Cameron didn't know where exactly his family was buried.

He tried to call, but she didn't answer. Ten minutes later, he parked behind the Charger. He hopped out as Steve's truck pulled up. His shoes sank into the grass as he walked toward his father's grave. Daron could see Aunt Bee off in the distance on her knees with Cameron comforting her. He approached them, but Cameron held her hand up. He stopped moving.

"It's my fault they're dead, Rook told me I shouldn't go back." Brandi ran her hand over the grey stone using her fingers to trace the name. "I snuck back because I had to tell Roger he wasn't going to get away with it."

Daron inched closer, careful to be as silent as possible. He wanted his aunt to continue talking.

"What did he do?" Cameron gently rubbed Brandi's back.

"Roger was using his daughter to traffick young girls."

Cameron's head snapped toward Daron, whose heart slammed in his chest.

"Darius was helping me move so that I'd have a safe place for Shane when he came back from visiting his father." Brandi turned, resting her back on the headstone and putting her focus on Daron. "But I should've listened to your father when he said we'd come back to help her later. I just couldn't stomach leaving her in that environment."

"What happened?" Daron lowered himself to the ground next to her, wrapping an arm around Brandi as she sobbed.

"I looked out the window," she replied between sniffles. "And I saw Roger's guy messing with your dad's car."

Daron couldn't believe what he was hearing. "Why didn't you stop him?"

"I tried, but by the time I reached the front porch, Roger was there. He held me back." Brandi's head dipped forward. "Roger and I fought. I raced up the stairs, trying to get to the phone but Roger yanked me down by the leg. By the time I managed to get away and to a phone ..."

"Dad wasn't answering."

Cameron left the two family members and stood next to Steve to give them some privacy.

"Everyone assumed he got in an accident coming home from Bishop's place." She pulled away from Daron and wiped her face with the palm of her hand. "He was on his way to pick up some groceries and supplies for me. Then he was supposed to swing back, grab my luggage, and drop me off at one of Bishop's spots."

Daron stood, then helped his aunt up from the grass. His mind reeled at the news. It was one thing to think his father died in a tragic accident but *to know* he was murdered. He needed a moment to process.

"Cam, would you mind taking my aunt home?" Daron maneuvered Brandi in the direction of the Charger.

Cameron wrapped both arms around him, squeezing him tightly. "Call me if you need me."

Steve approached him as they drove off. Both Daron and Steve's phones chimed simultaneously with an incoming text.

Reese and Amarion will be moved out of the city tomorrow night.

CHAPTER 24

Daron was grateful Cameron had come to the house after dropping Brandi off. They were able to create a plan to rescue Amarion and Reese while taking down the bad guys. They put together the piece of the puzzle he'd been overlooking.

Cameron called her brother Jason to assist simply to ensure they didn't get someone that had been bought off. The only way to pull this off was to use the Emperor's Suit. He'd called a meeting with the kings to get some much-needed help but he couldn't, in good conscience, let all them wear these suits worth billions if the tracker hadn't been installed. He made those last revisions and tweaks.

He entered the state-of-the-art conference room where coffee, tea, juice, and petite cut sandwiches graced a platter sitting on a wooden credenza. Daron had expected the credenza to be empty since this Castle meeting had not been planned in advance. The Kings were known for their healthy appetites for knowledge, building community, and good food.

"Is this emergency meeting about installing those protective shields?" Dro pulled out one of the navy executive chairs at the semi-circular conference table and dropped into it.

"No." Daron placed a laptop bag and a small duffle on the table. "I need help breaking into Marquise's mansion to save two of my young men." He was frustrated that Marquise was allowed to walk away.

"How do we know it isn't a setup?" Vikkas placed a steely gaze on Daron. "You did inherit your membership from a criminal."

Kaleb and Dwayne's heads snapped up from their devices and their gazes locked on Daron.

"I thought we'd moved past that."

"Past?" Vikkas shot back.

"Maybe we should talk about the reason you didn't mention that Kaleb was on property the day Khalil was shot." Daron glared at Vikkas, challenging him to say something else.

"Whoa, shit just got real," Jai said, sitting back in his chair.

"Hell, we didn't know any of that." Shaz put his elbows on the table and propped his head up on his hands. "I'm all ears."

"No. We'll have to deal with that topic another time." Daron grabbed the laptop bag off the conference table.

He only came to them instead of using his people because he thought they had a vested interest in taking Marquise and Adesh down. He had less than four hours to make this happen or he'd lose his window of opportunity. "I don't have time for this. We can discuss all that other stuff later. I have two young men to save and a couple of criminals to take down. All I need to know is who is in so I can stop wasting time."

Jai stood. "I'm in." But his gaze flickered between Kaleb and Vikkas

Dro, Reno, and Shaz joined Jai. Grant sauntered over to Vikkas as he headed toward the door.

Kaleb looked from Reno to Daron. "I'm sorry man. With everything going on, I can't afford for things to go wrong."

Dwayne rose to his feet. "You know I'm an educator. I have a little training from my time at Macro. I haven't done anything with it since then because that's not the circle I travel in. Your best option is to get people who are trained for this. Like the police or the FBI."

"They won't be the FBI's focus." Daron sat his projector on the conference table, scanning the faces of the men who remained.

The four men left The Castle's conference room, shutting the door behind them.

"We'll also be attempting to take down Adesh, who was key in bringing The Castle's security system down." Daron pulled the devices that compromised the foundation of The Suit and placed them on the table.

"Whoa." Shaz reared back in his seat. "Why wasn't he taken in with Terrell?"

"Because his motive doesn't seem to be money," Daron answered, "So we don't have proof he's involved."

"He's been head of security for almost as long as I know about The Castle." Jai shook his head.

Reno added, "Maybe with the shift in control of The Castle, he felt he had no other choice but to comply."

Dro typed something into a cell then stated, "Interrogating him could give us a clue on the motive behind the shooting or fill us in on some ..." He looked at where Kaleb had been sitting. "Other players."

Daron was thinking the same thing, that the information would put Dro on the right path to finding the mastermind.

A light knock came at the door and Roc peered in. "Calvin's here."

"Send him in," Daron instructed as he pulled up a 3-D holographic floor plan of Marquise's mansion, knowing they needed to focus on the current emergency, but by throwing suspicions on Kaleb and Vikkas he'd muddied the waters a little.

"His place has the same state-of-the-art security as The Castle," Dro explained, moving closer to the image.

"How do we get in?" Jai asked, studying the floor plan, tracing three of the exits with his index fingers.

"If Vikkas had allowed me to continue, he would have realized we'll be wearing suits, because its reflective and cloaking technology makes us invisible to the naked eye." Daron noted the disbelief in their eyes.

"Seriously," Shaz frowned. "How are we getting in? How is that even possible?"

"Walking through the doors." Daron gathered the items and opened up the laptop so that he could prepare to program the suits for their height and size.

"With those?" Reno collected two bracelets, glasses, and silver discs.

"Yes. You have the choice of wearing a hat." Daron held a thin, black skull cap out then touched the necklace. "Or this."

Reno pointed toward the gold-link necklace that matched the bracelets as Calvin entered the conference room.

"Perfect timing. Gentlemen, this is Calvin Atwood, the inventor of the device." Daron introduced Calvin to each man.

"Nice to meet you all," Calvin shook each of their hands as he made his way to Daron.

"He's here to help tailor the devices to you."

Daron let them choose between hat and necklaces.

Calvin picked up a silver disc. "These are very important. If you have a phone in your pocket and The Suit on, your phone can't be seen. However, if you take it out without this disc affixed to it, the phone will be seen."

"We'll be placing them on anything we might be using while the device is on." Daron placed one on his tablet. "Let me give you a demonstration."

He flicked the link on the bracelet on his right wrist and turned on the suit at the same moment the conference doors opened.

"We had a change of heart," Dwayne announced.

Daron didn't speak, curious about what the others would say when they realized what happened.

"Where did he go?" Grant asked, scanning the room as Kaleb and Vikkas followed him toward the conference table.

"He standing right in front of you." Dro chuckled, as he slipped on his bracelet.

Kaleb walked up to the conference table and stared at Marquise's mansion's floor plan.

"I thought he didn't have time to waste." Vikkas leaned on the wall, eyeing Calvin curiously.

"He was telling us how we're going to enter the mansion before you returned," Jai supplied.

"I was just demonstrating The Suit." Daron turned the device off and the four men's eyes widened. "As I was saying, this will get us through the doors undetected. The alarm will trigger, but they won't see anyone."

"Damn." Grant blinked twice, holding up the device Shaz handed him for closer inspection. "If I hadn't seen it for myself ..."

* * *

Daron needed all the men to enter the mansion at the same time to trigger the alarm. He had to get in place to record the transaction between Marquise and the recipient of the art and jewelry pieces. The team was dropped off at the edge of the property, just outside of the camera range, in vehicles driven by Steve, Vikkas, and Nicco. Daron signaled to activate the suits. Together they walked up the driveway. One guard was posted outside the door and four circled the grounds. Calvin, Mia, and Cameron were parked across the street monitoring the situation.

"Let me know when you're in position." Daron watched as Jai, Grant, Reno, and Kaleb made their way to the front door. He waited until the security team passed and headed to the security entrance.

"We're here," Jai announced.

"Same here," Dro, who was at the back entrance with Shaz, chimed in.

The guard checked his watch as Daron and Dwayne slid behind him.

"Go," Daron ordered, unlocked the door, then opened and closed it again after Dwayne cleared the threshold. The alarm blared, the man standing at the end of the hall placed a finger to his ear as if he was trying to listen from an earpiece.

A door opened and a man with ash-brown hair and a large belly looked around. "No one has come in or out?"

The blond guy at the end of the hall shrugged.

"It's unlocked," he asserted. "You're sure no one attempted to come out and changed their mind?" The man pulled the waistband up over his gut and stepped in with a hand near his firearm. The blond's only response was to look at him as though he was crazy. "Alright."

Daron and Dwayne sidestepped the guard as he searched the small alcove near the door.

"The system must be tripping." The guard gave a thumbs up to the blond man then returned to his position outside.

"We're all in," Dro said.

"We'll start our sweep," Shaz chimed in.

"I'll let you know when the cameras are down." Daron rushed to the security room, entering a code. It buzzed. *Incorrect*. He went to the next code. The green light appeared. Daron pushed the door open.

"What the hell?" Four men's heads snapped toward the door.

"Whoever's pulling pranks today of all days needs to cut it out," a man with a barrel chest standing in the center of the room said, before returning his attention to a large flat screen mounted on the wall. "It ain't funny."

Daron shot the three men in the chairs with a tranquilizer first, then when he was close enough to catch the remaining one, he took him out.

"What did you shoot them with?" Dwayne placed two fingers on one of the men's neck.

Daron handed Dwayne the gun, then collected the empty shells even though he knew they didn't contain fingerprints. "Something to put them to sleep while we work."

A door to the right opened, the security guard's eyes widened as he stared at his immobilized coworkers. Daron reached for his Beretta. Dwayne lifted the tranquilizer gun and hit the man in the shoulder. Moments later, the man's body hit the floor.

"Surprised you pulled the trigger." Daron gave a quick glance at the man writhing on the ground, then held out his fist for a pound.

Dwayne obliged, saying, "Even Jesus turned over a few tables in his days."

"Point taken." Daron shifted the guard onto his back so that he'd have feeling in his arm when he woke up. "But we're going to need to get you the same target practice as Milan," he said, referring to a shooting incident that occurred with Vikkas' woman. "That aim was off, bro."

Dwayne chuckled and rolled the man away from the center station and placed an empty seat in front of the security monitors. Daron stood at the supervisor's station.

"Okay, system down," Daron relayed so that all the Kings would know they could cut off The Suit when needed.

With a couple of keystrokes, Daron rerouted the feed to the room where the men were gathered into Jason's tablet and his own. The only camera recording was the room where Roger and Dr. Oakley were congregated. *Why is Roger here?* He pulled out the tablet, making sure the feed had come through then checked on Jai, Grant, Dro, Shaz, and Kaleb's progress.

"You know what you have to do." Daron left Dwayne monitoring the security team on the outside. He had wanted to take them down first, but Cameron had pointed out that it would definitely alert those monitoring the security. She reminded him that invisible or not, the men were solid mass that couldn't be "walked" through. Unfortunately, an increased security presence would make it difficult to navigate through the house.

"I'll let you know if they're any issues." Dwayne turned his attention to the screens.

Daron raced out, heading toward the entertainment room wondering where Marquise was as he listened to Dr. Oakley explaining how to administer the drug to keep Reese and Amarion out during transport and how young black boys were now in demand.

"We found Reese but we've got a problem," Kaleb announced.

"What kind of problem?" Daron changed direction, heading for the two men.

"We can't get to him," Reno explained.

He hit the hallway where the two security guys were laid out on the floor as Reno and Kaleb peered through the glass window in the door.

Reno twisted the knob. "Look at what happens when we attempt to open the door."

Daron watched as the back part of the floor lowered, opening as the chair Reese was bound and gagged to tilted back. He turned off his suit, scanning the area looking at the guards.

Kaleb frowned. "We checked them already."

Reese shook his head as Daron positioned his fingers in the okay symbol before they opened the door slightly to examine the inner panel. "What did you open the door with?"

A small black key-like device was extended. Daron attached it to the inner panel and the floor closed. "I suggest one of you go in and the other make sure this device stays in place."

"I *suggest* you don't step on the floor behind the kid," Reno stated as he replaced Daron in the threshold, giving Kaleb the task of getting Reese.

Kaleb shot Reno a dirty look as he entered the room.

"Daron, Levi's here," Cameron announced. "Coming through the front with one guy. Two more men are waiting outside the door."

"Dammit. Mia, I need to make sure Dwayne gets to his ride safely." Daron knew this situation could go sideways at any moment.

"I'm on it," Mia replied

Daron bolted toward the front, engaging The Suit knowing that there were still guards prowling around. A guard stepped into the hallway scanning the area, which caused Daron to pause until the man moved on. His suit started to flicker as he neared Bobby, Marquise, and Levi, who were arguing in the foyer.

"Calvin," Daron whispered as he pressed himself against the wall near a large display of statues. "My cloaking isn't working."

"Your main battery is low," Calvin replied. "Turn the activation link in the opposite direction to engage the backup battery."

Daron did as instructed and the issue stopped. He shifted position so he could see the three men.

"You didn't think I'd find out about this?" Levi asked.

"What is there to find out?" Marquise glanced down the hallway as if looking for someone. "I made the deal with the judge like you demanded."

"I didn't ask you to sell the one boy who saw me eliminate a mutual enemy to the judge," Levi fired back, pulling out a Glock.

"What do you think happens when you take over shit that ain't yours?" Marquise launched his thin body at Levi, surprising the two men.

Daron stood shocked as Marquise took Levi to the ground and choked him.

Bobby snatched Marquise off the larger man.

Levi hopped up and grabbed his gun off the floor.

"We'll see." Levi put a bullet in Marquise's leg and stuck the muzzle of his gun in the wound. Marquise let out a string of obscenities as his face contoured with the pain. "I'll be handling the transaction. Keep him in the living room. If Roger has a different tale to tell you're a dead man."

"Do we need to send one your way?" Mia asked.

"No," Daron replied as Bobby opened the door, letting two men in.

"Now show these two gentlemen where Amarion is or I will end you here." Levi pressed the gun against Marquise's forehead.

Levi's men grabbed Marquise as three guards ran into the foyer.

"We're fine," Levi said to the guards, who looked uncertain about walking away until Marquise nodded. They cautiously left the area as Marquise was escorted down the hallway, dragging one bloody leg.

Bobby and Levi headed to the back room.

"Guys, we're running out of time." Daron cursed, debating between following Levi or Marquise, then said, "Did you find Amarion?"

Once Levi made the payment, then the FBI would be coming through the door. No time to extract Amarion and get him to safety.

"One last area to check," Dro replied.

Jai's voice came through. "He's not in our area."

Daron checked his tablet to see Dro and Shaz still in the area Marquise was going. "Dro. Shaz. Trouble's headed your way." He followed Levi and prayed they would get to Amarion first.

Dr. Oakley and Roger, who sat on opposite ends of a long maroon couch, exchanged concerned looks as Levi entered the room.

"Where's Marquise and my money?" Dr. Oakley's eyes dropped to the gun in Levi's hand.

Levi replied, "I'll be handling things. The payment will be made soon."

An angry voice caught Daron's attention. "This isn't about money for me, I did it because Khalil lost his way and turned his back on The Castle and his—"

Daron slid into the bay across from the entertainment room that gave him a clear view of the meeting and Adesh, without blocking the entrance.

"Is that what you were told, you old fool?" Levi was laughing so hard, tears were sure to come. "Whoa, so gullible, no wonder I was told to recruit you."

Adesh's eyes widened and his mouth hung open. Clearly, he believed the lies.

"We found him," Shaz announced.

Daron watched as Adesh stormed out. "Jai and Grant, do you think you can detain Adesh until the FBI arrives?"

"We're on it," Grant replied.

Daron tapped the display screen of the tablet. Three men entered through the back, heading toward the entertainment room, passing Adesh along the way. Adesh stopped in his tracks as a table suddenly moved in his path. The older man dodged a cabinet door that kept opening and closing. Adesh raced to the door, struggling with the knob.

Daron refocused his attention on the entertainment room. Jai and Grant had the situation handled.

"You have them?" the newcomer asked, as the two henchmen stood behind him.

"Yes," Levi replied, then made a call. "Bring them in."

"Guys it's time to clear out," Daron announced.

He thought about Cameron's idea to cloak a vehicle and wished Calvin had made that a reality. Otherwise, he wouldn't be worried about them exiting the property. Only one vehicle would remain nearby and that one was Vikkas'.

"Adesh's tires are flat," Jai explained, with the humming of an engine in the background. "He's not going anywhere."

Daron moved further into the room to get a better look at the stranger, expecting to see someone else.

Roger stood as two men came in, one holding small briefcases and the other a poster tube by its strap and a small silver box.

"The Castle newbies won't be ready to take us on. We should keep hitting them where it hurts. Their personal lives" Levi took possession of the poster and silver box. "That's where they're most vulnerable."

The bald man with a trimmed beard seized the items, handing the box back while he examined the painting, then peeked into the silver box. "Once I get the document, I'll make sure there are no problems."

"Thanks, Judge." Levi extended a leather briefcase to Dr. Oakley, who quickly exited the room. "The injunction will stop their meddling right in its tracks."

Roger secured the other briefcase, along with the poster tube and silver box. "I'll transport them safely to your Phoenix property along with the boys."

"Speaking of the boys," Levi said.

"It's a setup," Dr. Oakley yelled in the distance.

The FBI had arrived.

The judge slowly inched out of the room. The judge's men whipped out their weapons. A bullet hit Roger in the shoulder as he bolted toward the door. He dropped everything in his hands. Bobby was hit twice and his body slammed against the floor. He dragged himself behind the couch. Levi returned fire, then sprinted down the hallway which led him straight into a group of agents.

The FBI entered, neutralizing the situation as Daron raced after Roger. "Vikkas, I'm coming your way and fast."

An engine roared to life. "I'm ready."

The older man was in better shape than he thought because Roger was on the front porch by the time Daron reached the foyer.

"Ugh."

Daron turned to see where the sound came from. Cameron had knocked an agent to the ground as he was about to take a shot at Roger. Only Daron would have taken the bullet since he had the cloaking engaged and was standing between the agent and Roger.

"Go," Cameron yelled, as Roger bolted down the stairs to a yellow Ferrari.

Daron sprinted around the truck and hopped in the passenger seat, noticing that the guards had been neutralized. He assumed courtesy of Cameron. Vikkas shot off after the Ferrari, his tires eating up the pavement.

"If this is supposed to be a high-speed chase, you know we're going to lose." Vikkas' hands were steady on the steering wheel as The Suburban sped down the driveway.

"He's probably trying to get to a doctor or hospital." At least that's what Daron hoped. A yellow sports car shouldn't be hard to track.

Roger paused, then pulled into the street.

Daron pulled out his phone to send a text to Mia. A loud boom and metal crushing snapped Daron's head toward the sound. The yellow vehicle became a blur. An eighteen-wheeler had hit the side and was pushing the Ferrari out of sight.

Vikkas hit the brakes and turned to Daron. "He's definitely going to the hospital."

CHAPTER 25

The missing piece of the puzzle fell into place when Brandi mentioned that Roger's daughter was helping him traffick girls from all over Chicago. Cameron reviewed a file Trenton had sent her on the young girl listed in Bishop's system as "Loretta A."

"You could give the info to your father since he clearly suspected Dr. Oakley of being up to something," Trenton suggested.

"So, you want *me* to tell him we've been following him," Cameron clapped back. She contemplated changing the meeting spot since she'd been waiting for almost ten minutes. *Jason should've been here by now.*

"Uh, no. Jason is a great choice." Trenton chuckled before ending the call.

Jason texted her forty-five minutes ago to say he was on the way, after she requested to see him. She glanced at the time on the dashboard again, wondering if he had trouble stepping away from the case at the office. Scanning the area, the same black Lexus that had driven away moments before Daron's guy got in position, rolled up the block and parked on the corner.

Cameron sighed, then used a device to shut down the community center's security camera and slid out the Charger. *It's going to be that type of night, I see.*

She positioned her body as if she was looking at the main street but kept her eyes on the woman creeping up on her in the shadows.

"They mentioned this was your favorite spot, but when I got the call that you were here, I couldn't believe my luck." Pebbles slid under the woman's feet as she stuck close to the brick wall, trying to stay out of the camera's range. "Do you know they tried to demote me from acquisitions to processing the girls because I didn't know Tracy wore a tracker? They even threatened me and tried to kill me once they found out I was trying to sell my service to someone else."

"Did I ask you for your life story?" Cameron turned toward the voice, positioning her hand near a weapon.

"Oh, but Daron came to my rescue. I should have known it was a setup when Bobby didn't just issue a threat and leave." Alisha stopped where the dirt met the sidewalk. "But he played the game well, shooting back as if Levi hadn't made it happen."

"Oh, so you're Queen Bee," Cameron said since Alisha seemed to have established her own set of followers. "I'm surprised that you're not with your father at the hospital."

"I'm trying to be Daron's queen since you don't seem up for the job." Alisha gave her a wicked smile. "And if that evil man, Roger, is in the hospital it means he finally got what he deserved."

"Daron and I are good." Cameron grabbed the wand in one hand and the gun in the other. "You and I, not so much."

Alisha advanced, pointing a Glock at Cameron with her other hand in the pocket of her jacket. "Don't move. My boys warned me about you."

"Evidently, you didn't listen to them. You picked the wrong time to come for me." She chuckled, knowing the bodysuit she wore would protect her unless Alisha shot at her head or hands. Then she'd have a big problem.

"If it's because Daron's expecting you at his place. Don't worry. I'll reappear in his life shortly after your funeral." Her facial expression was solemn even though her eyes were still lit with mischief. "A powerful man like that with a woman like me at his side, we'd be unstoppable."

"Daron's your power grab?"

Cameron shifted seconds before the gun fired a bullet that deflected off her arm. She slammed the wand across Alisha's weapon, then her face.

Alisha grunted as her other hand came out of her pocket with Mace, spraying.

Cameron knocked the can out of Alisha's hand but the mist hit the side of her face. She punched Alisha in the jaw, while her eyes burned. She and Alisha coughed as the Mace lingered heavily in the air. She swiped Alisha's feet from under her, then followed her to the ground. Cameron placed a Ruger in the center of Alisha's forehead as she wiped the mace from the side of her face using the jacket.

"Don't," Jason shouted.

"Lucky ass." Cameron backed up. She never intended to shoot her, at least not with a real bullet, maybe knock her out for a while. Her brother seemed to have a knack for coming in at the eleventh hour and making sure low life's survived.

Alisha reached for her ankle.

"But you're not." Alisha lifted the gun and pulled the trigger twice.

"No." Jason whipped out his weapon and shot Alisha in the chest.

The first bullet hit the wall just behind Cameron but the second one caught her in the gut. Cameron stumbled backward. Her shoulder hit the bricks as she felt the burn where the bullet hit. Jason kicked the gun away from Alisha's body then leaned over, feeling for a pulse.

Jason called for help, giving the location. He snatched Alisha's weapon from the ground and rushed over to Cameron. "Is this your idea of retirement?"

"Retirement hurts," Cameron murmured. "If I was planning to do dirt, do you really think I'd invite my FBI brother to the party?" Cameron was glad she was doing Daron a favor this evening. Otherwise, she wouldn't have been dressed for the occasion.

"Did you think I was going to shoot you?" Jason lifted her jacket to see the bullet wedged into her armored jumpsuit.

"Let's just say I've been getting a lot of unexpected visitors." Cameron didn't want to tell him that she was on the premises when he arrived to take down Levi, Marquise, and the dirty judge.

"Could it be that you're dating a suspected criminal?" Jason stared at the bullet lodged in the brick.

"This trouble has nothing to do with his past and everything to do with him tracking down that missing girl, when law enforcement couldn't." Cameron didn't want to mention The Castle. Jason would think Daron was working with the criminal element and want to bring him to justice. She couldn't have her brother getting in Daron's way.

"Damn Cam, how about you take some time to focus on your new facility?"

Cameron kept her eye on Alisha, since there was movement in her chest, although faint. "You want me with him."

"What?" His face crinkled into a scowl as his hazel eyes narrowed. "Why do you say that?"

Cameron snickered. "You shot my biggest competition."

"If I'd known *that*, I wouldn't have. I'm going to keep her ass alive by any means necessary." Jason ripped off his jacket and used it to apply pressure to Alisha's wound, scanning the area. "Where is that damn ambulance?"

Cameron chuckled at the seriousness etched in his face. "Before your people arrive, I was trying to give you the lead on Miss Alisha there and a few more individuals." Cameron pulled out the baggie and opened it so he could grab the flash drive.

The siren sounded closer. "Don't go anywhere. I can't make this disappear and I need you to get checked out."

"How am I supposed to explain the Kevlar?" Cameron looked back at the wall. At least he could say Alisha took a shot at him and an informant, which would be technically true.

"Go." He slipped the flash drive into his pocket and returned to applying pressure.

"Let's do lunch." Cameron moved toward the Charger. "I need to talk to you about dad."

Jason's jaw dropped, but he didn't get a word out before she disappeared.

CHAPTER 26

The news that Alisha was the little girl Brandi was trying to help came as a shock to Daron. The fact that Roger threatened to traffick her if she didn't assist was appalling. Now Levi's statement about causing him to lose money made sense, especially since Marquise and Roger were really working for him.

They transported Marquise's stolen merchandise to clients, along with drugs, Roger's illegal wares and trafficking victims. The entire situation made Daron sick to his stomach. The leads Daron's team had on the shooter Marquise hired, hadn't panned out. He turned the task over to Red, hoping he'd have better luck.

"Cam's father can cross Dr. Oakley off his list." Nicco sat a whiskey mule on a square wooden table next to Daron's tablet.

"Hopefully, the other doctors on the list are not like Oakley."

Bringing Dr. Oakley and Marquise to justice made Daron realize his life would be entangled with that of these eight other directors of The Castle for the foreseeable future. Might as well take the time to really get to know them outside of their scheduled meetings.

"You picked a beautiful day to have a barbecue," Nicco said, reaching into the small refrigerator to grab some fruit. "Is Cam coming?"

"Calvin and Mia, too." Daron figured The Castle would be the best place to host the event.

Daron hoped spending time with the Kings would give Cameron an opportunity to talk with them and accept that they were not criminals. Her silence didn't mean she wasn't still questioning his retirement and new responsibilities. He'd already messed up their relationship by projecting his fears on her and focusing more on his purpose, as if it had been an 'either-or' scenario. She had a right to be concerned.

"Did Pedro get the boys settled?" Nicco asked, sitting the orange slices, pineapple chunks, and cherries on the counter.

"Yeah. We have JD helping Amarion and Reese get set up in New York, while Pedro's in DC getting Cedric squared away."

Daron lowered the silver lid on the grill, then sat down. The early morning start had begun to take its toll. He reached for the glass of whiskey as the tablet chimed.

Nicco grabbed the Glock tucked in the waistband of his shorts, hidden under the tank top. "Which quadrant?"

Daron picked up the device and shook his head. "It's Cam."

The only reason he knew Cameron was coming was because he installed sensors on the exterior wall that were hard to see from a distance. Daron still had some work to do on security. She shouldn't have gotten this close to the building without him being notified. He wondered if she'd come in on a motorcycle. She was wearing a jogging suit with a backpack and baseball cap low on her forehead. By the time she made it to the end of the building, Daron was waiting for her.

"You're hiding again, gorgeous." He tugged on her cap before pulling her into his arms and giving her a peck on the lips.

"Of course not," she replied, following him into the backyard.

The sun beamed down on them as she walked beside Daron through the uncovered seating area with a fire pit waiting to be lit, moving closer to the smoky-sweet smell.

Cameron waved to Nicco, who was back to manning the bar that had stools inside and outside the pool. Her eyes stayed on Nicco too long. Daron assumed she was checking out his tattoo sleeve which was normally hidden under suits. *At least, that had better be why.*

Daron placed a hand on her lower back and guided her into the covered kitchen. She walked over to the fireplace that held the large screen television where there was more outdoor furniture. He imagined that sitting outside with the fireplace going on cooler days was a great way to wind down. A mix of R&B, oldies and Jazz played in the background.

"You're the grill master for today." Cameron smiled as she returned to his side near the pit. "I thought the staff would handle that."

"To ensure there was no drama and everyone could safely enjoy getting to know each other. I chose to cook and put Nicco on drinks." Daron pointed toward the pool with a rock waterfall feature. "We have Linc as the lifeguard."

Cameron waved at Linc, who was relaxing in a chair on a landing with a fire pit that seemed to float on the pool's lily pad. Linc walked over to the patio side heading their way.

Nicco slid from behind the bar.

"How about I watch the grill while you give her a tour," Nicco offered, entering the kitchen.

Linc replaced Nicco at the bar.

"Sounds good." Daron pointed to the stairs near where the water cascaded down. "There's a private whirlpool up there."

He walked her down the path that led to the basketball courts, tennis courts, then toward the golf course. Daron directed her attention to his left. "Further back there is a lake and stables."

"I imagine the area near the lake is serene and beautiful," Cameron stated, as they strolled down the path. "It's a lot of estate to protect."

He captured her hand in his, then stopped moving. "Your comment that I can't be your King and a King of The Castle stuck with me."

"Don't ruin the day by starting an argument." Cameron tugged him forward.

He held her waist, guiding her to one of the benches along the path where they sat down. "I admit that I didn't handle the discovery of my membership in the correct way. At the time, I felt the best method to maintain our relationship was to wait until I found out more."

He had to admit to himself that the decision had more to do with how he thought she would react to the news than her actual actions, which were reasonable given the circumstances.

"That doesn't sound like the relationship we discussed that we'd build on honesty." Cameron ran a hand through her reddish-brown hair. "I don't want to feel like I'm on one of Bishop's assignments in my personal life."

"Don't walk away without at least giving us a real chance." Daron held her hand as she stood. "I love you."

Cameron stared at him but said nothing. He could see she was debating with herself.

Daron immediately felt numb. Was she actually planning on permanently cutting ties with me? "What is it?"

"To be honest, I wish you weren't involved in The Castle. My entire point of wanting to be sure you remained retired was so we could maintain the life we had *before* you received that call from Katara."

The sadness in her eyes was a gut punch. Even though he expected Cameron to be stubborn and difficult, Daron had been so sure he'd get her back. However, he hadn't counted on the fact that with the membership there was no returning to how they were before the call. "Babe, your friends are *actual* criminals and you see them on a regular basis."

She raised an eyebrow. "It's not them that my mom is asking to meet."

"Accept the role of Queen in my life and let me show you that we can find the same kind of happiness in our new norm." Daron slid his arms around her waist, gazing into her eyes. "Together we'll work on implementing the same precautions that your father and brothers have, to keep work-life from crossing over to their personal one. Can we do that?"

Cameron paused, taking a deep breath. Her hesitation made him slightly nervous.

"Yes. But no more ultimatums."

"Be warned," he said, placing his forehead on hers. "I'm going to be on you about speaking to your father. I feel like you were able to walk away without blinking an eye because of your relationship with him."

"I did blink an eye." She smirked. "I can't help if you missed it."

Daron chuckled before lowering his mouth to hers, tasting what he'd been craving since she'd tossed back the house keys. "Making us official feels so right."

"I'll deal with you harassing me about Jake, but this time you'll have to mean what you say, Daron. We're a team." She placed a palm against his face with her brown eyes laser-focused on him. "No making decisions that affect both our lives without so much as a mention."

He wrapped her in both arms holding her firmly as she laid her head on his shoulder. "Moving forward, I'll honor the team." Closing his eyes, he reveled in the feel of her body against his, praying that they would develop a foundation strong enough to handle the truths about his past decisions.

She broke the embrace and her full lips curled into a smile. "Your woman is hungry from the hike she had to take to get to this shindig."

"I'm hungry for another type of nutrition." He pulled her back into his growing erection.

"You better eat well now because tonight we have a lot of lost time to make up for." She slid a hand across his bulge, gently caressing as she slowly sucked his bottom lip before her tongue began exploring his mouth.

"Damn." Daron wished he didn't know how many drones and cameras were on the property, otherwise, he wouldn't be waiting for tonight.

Reluctantly he broke the embrace, leading her back to the outdoor kitchen. He relieved Nicco from grill duties as Cameron washed her hands, then set out the plates and cutlery. She snagged a turkey hotlink from the traditional barbecue pan on the stand next to the macaroni and cheese and dirty rice. He peeled back the plastic so she could use the tongs to grab the chips.

"Do you think I should put the other items out?" Daron asked, opening the small refrigerator and lifting out the salad to see if she wanted any.

She shook her head. "Wait at least until someone else arrives, the sun isn't playing with anybody today."

Daron joined her at the table after flipping the vegetables on the grill.

Being there talking with Cameron reminded him of his mother sitting with his father as he finished barbecuing. She'd once told Daron after getting up so early, his father would be tired and she'd keep him talking until he got his second wind.

We should have had more time, Dad.

Cameron rested her hand on his shoulder. "Are you okay?"

"Yeah. Just thinking I'm grateful that if Roger survives, he'll be prosecuted for his crimes." His tablet beeped, but he knew Nicco and Linc were watching the security feeds. "And that Ralph, has had the charges dropped."

She slid an arm around his shoulder, pulling him closer and planting a kiss on his cheek.

"He did handle the entire situation with dignity and grace though some people will always think he was involved." Daron rested a hand on her thigh, appreciating that this moment was the first time he felt that maybe happiness didn't have to be an occasional visitor in this new life. "I'm planning to refer the youth I come across to Tony while I widen my net for a candidate to run my program."

A few minutes later, Reno and Kaleb arrived, then Grant moments later. Daron introduced Cameron, who gave them an intense once over and directed them to the food.

"Are you cooking for an army?" Grant asked as he approached the long table filled with chafing dishes. He peeked into three warming units that contained either lamb chops, jerked chicken or rib-eye with lime Tequila butter.

"What we don't eat, we box and deliver to the homeless," Daron stated, as he fixed a plate with fruit and cheese to snack on. "Besides, y'all left Dwayne's house on empty the first time we showed up?"

"Weren't you the one who was the first to the table?" Kaleb asked.

"See, why you want to bring up old shit?"

His brothers laughed. So did Cameron, before heading to the bar to get a drink.

"What's this?" Reno asked pointing to the last chafer as Shaz and Dro arrived.

Dro looked a little worn-out, probably because his crisis management clients kept him on high octane adventures.

"Grigliata mista di carne. I think." Daron reached for a piece of fruit, but Cameron returned and commandeered the plate.

"You think." Grant chuckled, peeking in the chafer with corn on the cob, salmon with Bourbon glaze, and Cajun shrimp skewers.

"Hey, it's technically a platter of mixed grilled meats, but I don't know if Italians would say it qualified as Grigliata mista di carne." Daron removed the last of the veggie kabobs and the assorted vegetables from the grill.

"We'll see," Reno said, making his way down to the end of the line.

"As long as it tastes as good as it looks." Kaleb picked up a plate. "I don't care what it's called."

"Coleslaw, Potato Salad, and cold items are in the refrigerator," Daron carried the salad and dressings to the table as Dwayne and his girlfriend, Tiffany, made their way over, followed by Calvin and Mia.

Daron made introductions.

Jai, and a woman they barely knew, arrived a few minutes after Cameron and Mia left to change to hit the pool. "I see you all got started without me." He scanned the plates of food, but the pressure of dealing with the fallout from the discovery that a comatose patient at his clinic was pregnant was clearly etched on his face.

"Did you get my proposal for adding a weight alarm to the bed with safe zone sensors along sides of the bed?" Daron asked.

Jai lifted his cell, smiled then said, "Thanks."

Daron hoped it helped prevent a repeat of the incident in the future. Now Jai had to survive the physical and emotional fallout of the investigation. Daron glanced at Vikkas and Milan as they approached the group. "Why is it that the person who actually *lives* on the property is the last to arrive?"

"You can't make an entrance if you're first to the party," Vikkas announced as he guided Milan past the square tables to the long one where everyone was dining.

Daron made his way to Reno, who looked relaxed even though he was dealing with the surge in crime and how it affected his women's shelter. He also had the added headache of someone hunting for a Tanzanian princess at the shelter, who was trying to remain out of the clutches of a father who'd sold her like a piece of meat. "Did you get all the evaluation forms in for the women?"

The new process would determine whether the women could receive the tracking earrings or they'd have to come up with an alternative.

Reno's jaw clenched as he ran a hand through his hair. "I'm curious. What would be the alternative?"

"A bracelet, maybe a ring or watch." Daron thought about Tracy. Her experience would have been very different if the traffickers had known to take out the earrings. "However, if Pedro deemed any of them unstable, in good conscience, he couldn't give them any device."

"Once they are approved, they'll receive a device and the membership to receive training?" Reno queried.

Daron gestured to the women chatting it up with Cameron. "If you have any questions, it's a perfect opportunity to speak with Mia, who will be in charge of transportation and Cameron, who will be handling training." Daron glanced at Cameron and Mia, who took a few laps between talking with Linc poolside and Nicco at the bar.

He was thankful she was wearing one of her more conservative swimsuits. Daron was already contemplating how to slip out so he could feel those thick thighs wrapped around him.

"You okay over there?" Reno glanced at him, then looked at the pool before returning his attention to Daron.

Daron focused on the table. "Yeah."

Cameron slipped into a purple and silver sundress cover-up, then made her way back to the group. He introduced her to the remaining people. Despite the fact that they all were going through some major challenges, they seemed to be enjoying themselves.

Kaleb was still caught up in the investigation into the suspicious arson of his property, resulting in the death of several young women. Grant was being blackmailed for something he did when getting his business off the ground. He wasn't aware Daron knew, but Daron planned to stay out of it unless Grant asked for help.

Calvin took a seat next to Daron. "This is a great break from working. Thanks for the invite."

"No problem." Daron knew the next few weeks would be extremely busy with them testing how the tracker affected The Suits in different environments. The Kings were determined to help out. "Enjoy. We'll be back to the grind in a couple of days."

Dwayne went to the bar while Daron downed his whiskey and decided it was time for another drink.

"How are things?" Daron lowered himself onto a bar stool.

Dwayne picked up the drinks Nicco placed on the counter. "I'm adjusting."

He was obviously struggling with the shift from life as a professor to the issues and dangers that came with being a King, while still balancing his vision for his charter school. That night at Marquise's mansion showed he was up for the challenge.

"Well, I've only had a taste of the life you were living before The Castle dropped in the mix, shaking things up. I have moments where I crave the return of the peace and stability, but I know if we—" Daron nodded at the men laughing and talking around the table. "—restore this place to its original purpose, lives will be changed for the better. Including ours, and we won't regret this leap of faith."

He patted Dwayne on the back, took his own drink from Nicco, and they headed back to the group.

Khalil was approaching, with Steve as his personal guard. Daron was slightly surprised Khalil had made an appearance since his schedule stayed busy.

Cameron seemed to be enjoying herself and wasn't faking it for his benefit.

Reno, Shaz, Dro, and Kaleb had moved to the table that held the decks of cards and were playing bid whist, another game Khalil taught them in school.

Daron walked over, sliding an arm around Cameron's waist as she watched the men laughing, talking trash, and slapping down cards. He was confident he could make this new tribe work. Life didn't always go as planned, but unexpected blessings always managed to slip in and make an appearance.

"What are you thinking?" Cameron asked.

"That we need to make a quiet exit, so I can not only show you my wing of The Castle, but also how much I've missed you." Daron took her hand, slipping away to demonstrate that the beauty and splendor of The Castle paled in comparison to the love he had for her.

You met Calvin and Mia in *King of Morgan Park*. They actually have their own story in T*he Confection Assignment* where you'll learn more about the making of the Emperor's Suit.

Mia's head snapped up at a sound that wasn't anything like the faint echoes of music from the other end of the lake. For some reason, her instinct was on high alert especially since the additional security team was missing in action.

"Having dinner out here was a great idea," Mia said for the sake of their nosy neighbor Patty, who was walking in their direction as Calvin approached the table.

The older woman wasn't any cause for concern.

"You like me cooking for you." He brought out the spaghetti and salad, slid it on the table, then leaned in, kissing Mia. He wrapped his arm around her waist, nuzzling her neck. "Maybe we should have dessert first."

"I'll not be reheating dinner tonight." Pushing him away, she turned him back toward the house, then swatted that gorgeous rear end of his to send him on his way. "You need to go grab those breadsticks. I'll open the wine."

Calvin, who had never been married, enjoyed playing the role of husband a little too much. He winked before stepping off the planks and into the dining room. He paused at the door and glanced over his shoulder. "We need to do this more often."

Most often wouldn't happen. Tonight was the last day of her assignment, then she'd be back to her regular life and that didn't include being a high security detail protector to a top secret invention and its handsome creator.

Several minutes later, she poured him a glass of red wine before fixing their plates. She scanned the area again and a tingle of suspicion ignited in her mind.

What's taking him so long?

"Calvin, today would be nice," Mia yelled. She perched on the chair, waiting for his smart response.

None came.

Mia placed the glass on the table and swept into the house. Calvin wasn't in the kitchen. If he had slipped into his office to work instead of joining her outside, there was going to be a problem.

Mia laid eyes on Calvin as she rounded the corner, but his voice halted her in her tracks.

"Run, Mia. Run," Calvin yelled, lunging for the stocky Asian man near the office door.

A hefty Black guy slammed his weapon across the back of Calvin's head.

Mia sprinted down the hallway past the study and powder room, aiming to get her weapon. She kicked herself for not bringing it inside. They wouldn't kill Calvin, but they could hurt him if he didn't cooperate. She slid a cast iron skillet from the cooktop.

"Go get her," someone yelled from the office.

Several things crashed to the office floor. Calvin put up one hell of a fight. Mere seconds had passed when Mia's pursuer rounded the corner. She slammed the skillet into his chest, causing him to fly into the wall. He recovered and reached for her arm. The skillet crashed down onto his head with a backward swipe. This time, his body hit the ground, right on top of his gun.

Damn.

Her feet pounded on the hardwood floor as she raced for the front entrance, aiming to find some type of reinforcements. An armed man came off the path to the porch. She slammed the front door, locking it. Keys jiggled in the tumbler.

Mia ran top speed toward the kitchen ahead of a spray of bullets that landed in the cabinets. She slid toward the island like a baseball player trying to reach the home plate. She scrambled around the counter, bolting to the deck and made it to the table.

"Nowhere to run," a man with an ivory complexion said as a Latino guy calmly stepped over the threshold onto the deck as though nothing out of the ordinary had transpired.

"Don't be so sure of that." She snatched the Ruger, aimed, and pulled the trigger five times taking out the biggest threat. Mia didn't wait for the Latino man's advancing body to hit the ground. She hit the stairs. The ivory man took cover in the dining room and held up on a perfect vantage spot.

Three armed men raced toward her. Damn, how many did they send?

Her heart sank, but adrenaline kicked in as she turned back.

She had to make it to the Lincoln.

"Mrs. Atwood, don't do it," he yelled as she climbed from the patio chair to the railing.

He aimed his Glock and fired.

Mia took a flying leap from the banister and dove into the water.

Daron and Cameron had an interesting life before The Castle. Their story is told in *Transition of Power.*

Most days Cameron Stone was an upstanding citizen. Nights, not so much. She spent those reclaiming stolen items and returning them to their previous owners for a hefty fee. For owners who couldn't make a police report for items from their private collection of stolen properties purchased off the black market. This, along with other things, was one of many assignments she and her team, Greg, Rob, and Trenton had when she worked for a man named Bishop who dabbled in all things illegal. Today she was doing recon in downtown Chicago, preparing for a job they would execute later that evening.

People milled about on their lunch, soaking up the touch of warm weather before the Chicago chill returned. Cameron placed a manicured hand on top of her fake pregnant belly as she sat in the outdoor seating at Pub on Wabash Street. The view of a particular stony office building, not the food, had brought her there. She carefully scanned the area.

"Need anything else?" the waitress asked, picking up the cash payment Cameron had left for the bill.

"No. Thanks," Cameron replied, shifting the wicker chair toward the black metal gate fencing around the seating area.

Her gaze was focused on the door where the client would exit but her mind was on leaving the business. She wasn't convinced it was the right time, especially given the latest incident of someone snatching their product before it was delivered to the client. She did a double take as a woman passed her who bore a striking resemblance to Kathleen Stone, one of the few women Bishop allowed into their inner circle.

Cameron's cell vibrated. She slid the handsfree buds into her ears as her eyes shifted to the bald man with a beer belly hanging over his belt, stepping out of the dull brown office building. Her client, Mr.

Arthur, was on the move. Being a creature of habit was dangerous. She already knew what restaurant he was heading to and what he'd order.

She answered Rob's call. "Hey hon, I'm sorry. Got your message. It's okay to place the order."

"Greg is calling him now," Rob replied.

Cameron increased the volume to tune out the chatter of the older couple sitting nearby, the city sounds and the rumbling of the train overhead. The light changed and Mr. Arthur crossed the street. She could hear the client answer. A tall spiky-haired man walked past Mr. Arthur, blocking her view of his mouth. She watched chubby man continue his journey without a cell in his hand.

"We may have a problem," Cameron said as she rose to her feet, waddling down the street. She reached him before he made it to the building that housed Heaven on Seven. He had no hands-free set and Greg was still on the line with the client. Who was pretending to be him? "Track the caller's location now."

The Gu, a 12th Century metal piece, was one of thirteen works stolen from the Gardner Museum in 1990, had been in Mr. Arthur's possession from a black-market purchase. FBI offered a ten-million-dollar reward by for recovery the Museum's thirteen pieces. They were worth more on the black market. Someone had stolen it from Mr. Arthur, killing his wife in the process. The police report corroborated the break-in and murder and Cameron had a feeling that old man missed his artwork more than his wife. She had let herself into his private museum which was hidden behind the bar in his basement. Pictures with him standing next to the Gu were splayed in the vault, but barely any around of his deceased wife. The client, who stated he had located the Gu and wanted it retrieved, was clearly not Mr. Arthur.

One thing she learned from her first failed job was expect to be double-crossed and be prepared for anything.

Karen D. Bradley

is a national bestselling author for her contribution to the NKTCS Sugar anthology. English and Grammar were never her strongest subjects. As life would have it, her weakest link would become her saving grace. Writing fiction became one of her favorite forms of therapy and kept her sane through life's ups and downs. She has penned several contemporary fiction and suspense novels. Venturing into film making, she wrote and produced a short film based on one of her novels. Visit Karen on the web at www.karendbradley.com or on Twitter, Instagram and Pinterest @ms_kbradley.

ABOUT THE KINGS OF THE CASTLE SERIES

Books 2-9 are standalones, no cliffhangers, and can be read in any order.

Book 1 – Kings of the Castle, the introduction to the series and story of King of Wilmette (Vikkas Germaine)

USA TODAY, *New York Times*, and National Bestselling Authors work together to provide you with a world you'll never want to leave. The Castle. Powerful men unexpectedly brought together by their pasts and current circumstances will become a force to be reckoned with. Their combined efforts to find the people responsible for the attempt on their mentor's life, is the beginning of dangerous challenges that will alter the path of their lives forever. Not to mention, they will also draw the ire and deadly intent of current Castle members who wield major influence across the globe.

Fate made them brothers, but protecting the Castle and the women they love, will make them Kings. www.thekingsofthecastle.com

King of Chatham - Book 2 - Reno
King of Evanston - Book 3 - Shaz
King of Devon - Book 4 - Jai
King of Morgan Park - Book 5 - Daron
King of South Shore - Book 6 - Kaleb
King of Lincoln Park - Book 7 - Grant
King of Hyde Park - Book 8 - Dro
King of Lawndale - Book 9 - Dwayne

Cover design by J. L. Woodson - www.woodsonstudio.com

ABOUT THE KINGS OF THE CASTLE SERIES

Books 2-9 are standalones, no cliffhangers, and can be read in any order.

Book 1 – Kings of the Castle, the introduction to the series and story of King of Wilmette (Vikkas Germaine)

USA TODAY, *New York Times*, and National Bestselling Authors work together to provide you with a world you'll never want to leave. The Castle. Powerful men unexpectedly brought together by their pasts and current circumstances will become a force to be reckoned with. Their combined efforts to find the people responsible for the attempt on their mentor's life, is the beginning of dangerous challenges that will alter the path of their lives forever. Not to mention, they will also draw the ire and deadly intent of current Castle members who wield major influence across the globe.

Fate made them brothers, but protecting the Castle and the women they love, will make them Kings.

www.thekingsofthecastle.com

King of Chatham - Book 2

While Mariano "Reno" DeLuca uses his skills and resources to create safe havens for battered women, a surge in criminal activity within the Chatham area threatens the women's anonymity and security. When Zuri, an exotic Tanzanian Princess, arrives seeking refuge from an arranged marriage and its deadly consequences, Reno is now forced to relocate the women in the shelter, fend off unforeseen enemies of The Castle, and endeavor not to lose his heart to the mysterious woman.

King of Evanston - Book 3

Raised as an immigrant, he knows the heartache of family separation firsthand. His personal goals and business ethics collide when a vulnerable woman stands to lose her baby in an underhanded and profitable scheme crafted by powerful, ruthless businessmen and politicians who have nefarious ties to The Castle. Shaz and the Kings of the Castle collaborate to uproot the dark forces intent on changing the balance of power within The Castle and destroying their mentor. National Bestselling Author, J.L. Campbell presents book 3 in the Kings of the Castle Series, featuring Shaz Bostwick.

King of Devon - Book 4

When a coma patient becomes pregnant, Jaidev Maharaj's medical facility comes under a government microscope and media scrutiny. In the midst of the investigation, he receives a mysterious call from someone in his past that demands that more of him than he's ever been willing to give and is made aware of a dark family secret that will destroy the people he loves most.

King of Morgan Park - Book 5

Two things threaten to destroy several areas of Daron Kincaid's life— the tracking device he developed to locate victims of sex trafficking and an inherited membership in a mysterious outfit called The Castle. The new developments set the stage to dismantle the relationship with a woman who's been trained to make men weak or put them on the other side of the grave. The secrets Daron keeps from Cameron and his inner circle only complicates an already tumultuous situation caused by an FBI sting that brought down his former enemies. Can Daron take on his enemies, manage his secrets and loyalty to the Castle without permanently losing the woman he loves?

King of South Shore - Book 6

Award-winning real estate developer, Kaleb Valentine, is known for turning failing communities into thriving havens in the Metro Detroit area. His plans to rebuild his hometown neighborhood are dereailed with one phone call that puts Kaleb deep in the middle of an intense criminal investigation led by a detective who has a personal vendetta. Now he will have to deal with the ghosts of his past before they kill him.

King of Lincoln Park - Book 7

Grant Khambrel is a sexy, successful architect with big plans to expand his Texas Company. Unfortunately, a dark secret from his past could destroy it all unless he's willing to betray the man responsible for that success, and the woman who becomes the key to his salvation.

King of Hyde Park - Book 8

Alejandro "Dro" Reyes has been a "fixer" for as long as he could remember, which makes owning a crisis management company focused on repairing professional reputations the perfect fit. The same could be said of Lola Samuels, who is only vaguely aware of his "true" talents and seems to be oblivious to the growing attraction between them. His company, Vantage Point, is in high demand and business in the Windy City is booming. Until a mysterious call following an attempt on his mentor's life forces him to drop everything and accept a fated position with The Castle. But there's a hidden agenda and unexpected enemy that Alejandro doesn't see coming who threatens his life, his woman, and his throne.

King of Lawndale - Book 9

Dwayne Harper's passion is giving disadvantaged boys the tools to transform themselves into successful men. Unfortunately, the minute he steps up to take his place among the men he considers brothers, two things stand in his way: a political office that does not want the competition Dwayne's new education system will bring, and a well-connected former member of The Castle who will use everything in his power—even those who Dwayne mentors—to shut him down.

AUTHOR BIOS

Naleighna Kai is the *USA TODAY* Bestselling Author of Every Woman Needs a Wife, Open Door Marriage, Loving Me for Me, Slaves of Heaven and several other controversial novels. She is founder of NK Tribe Called Success, The Cavalcade of Authors, and is a publishing and marketing consultant. www.naleighnakai.com

S. L. Jennings is a military wife, mom of three, coffee addict, Willy Wonka enthusiast, and real-life unicorn. She's also the New York Times and USA Today Bestselling author of Taint, Fear of Falling and the Se7en Sinners Series, along with a few other titles that she's too lazy to type. She's been with her high school sweetheart for almost twenty years, and he still can't get her Subway sandwich order right. But he's cute and brings her vodka, so she keeps him around. They currently reside in Spokane, WA with their three stinky boys and their equally stinky cat. www.sljenningsauthor.com

Martha Kennerson is the bestselling and award-winning author who's love of reading and writing is a significant part of who she is. She uses both to create the kinds of stories that touch the heart. Martha lives with her family in League City, Texas. She believes her current blessings are only matched by the struggle it took to achieve such happiness. To find out more about Martha and her journey, visit her website at www.marthakennerson.com and you can follow her on Facebook and Twitter.

J. L. Campbell is an award-winning Jamaican author who has written over thirty books in several romance subgenres. Campbell, who features Jamaican culture in her stories, is a certified editor, and also writes non-fiction. Visit her on the web at www.joylcampbell.com.

National bestselling author, **Lisa Watson**, is a native of Washington D.C., and writes in the Multicultural & Interracial, Contemporary, Romantic Suspense, and Sweet Romance genres. Her memorable novels for the Harlequin's Kimani line, The Match Broker series was listed as one of 2014's Top 25 Books of the Summer, and Top 50 Best Reads. Lisa lives in Raleigh, North Carolina with her husband of twenty-two years and two teenagers, and is avidly working on book one, Alexa King: The Guardian, in her second new Romantic Suspense series, The Lady Doyen and Book 2 in the Love and Danger Series. www.lisawatson.com

Karen D. Bradley is a national bestselling author and screenplay writer. English and Grammar were never her strongest subjects, but as life would have it, her weakest link would become her saving grace. Writing fiction became one of her favorite forms of therapy. She has penned several contemporary fiction, suspense, and romantic suspense novels. Visit Karen on the web at www.karendbradley.com

Janice M. Allen is a National Bestselling Author who has always been an avid reader of fiction. She even edited the work of other authors for several years. But she gets an incomparable thrill from creating stories that entertain readers and cause them to reflect on real life issues. No Right Way To Do A Wrong Thing is her first novel, followed by her short story Cayenne. www.janicemallen.com

London St. Charles has always had a passion for the pen, paper, and books. She is a Chicago native who uses the Windy City as a backdrop to the romance, suspense, and contemporary fiction stories she writes. London published her debut novel, The Husband We Share in 2017 and is one of nine authors in the anthology, Sugar. She also composes an online newsletter, London Writes, that keeps readers abreast of what's going on in her world. www.londonstcharles.com

MarZe Scott is a lifelong resident of Ypsilanti, Michigan and Graduate of University of Michigan. A lover of all things creative, MarZé enjoys reading, free-hand illustrating, jewelry making and makeup artistry.

Known for her vivid and captivating storytelling, MarZé has been writing short stories and poems since elementary school and developed a taste in high school for writing about provocative topics like the consequences of casual sex. You can find Gemini Rising, MarZé's debut novel, and short story Next Lifetime wherever books are sold. www. marzescott.com

SERIES MENTORS:

LaVerne Thompson is a *USA Today* Bestselling, award winning, multi-published author, an avid reader and a writer of contemporary, fantasy, and sci/fi sensual romances. She loves creating worlds within and without our world. She also writes romantic suspense and new adult romance under the pen name Ursula Sinclair also a USA Today Bestselling Author. www.lavernethompson.com

Kassanna is a strong believer in love at first sight and happily ever afters. Writing has always been her passion but fate sometimes has other roads that must first be taken .Navigating the road less traveled was not only unexpected but in the end extremely rewarding. Her books are mainly contemporary romance but she has delved into the paranormal, fantasy, and plans on expanding into other areas as the ideas come to her. Right now she is enjoying life and seeing her works come into fruition make it that much more pleasurable especially when her books make others smile. Kassanna wouldn't have it any other way. www. flavorfullove.com